RESONANT
LIVES

RESONANT LIVES

K.S.K. EBBAGE

ISBN 978-1-7397244-0-5

Perhaps the destiny of everything - ever, is just sitting there - like in a natural cyberspace…

Chapter One

We all love the thrill of watching a classic scientific experiment. To some, it's Victorian magic, smoke, bangs and lightning - it's timeless. Most of us though, have never questioned why some of these scientific breakthroughs - seemingly, have never really found a use for the benefit of the world.

There is one name in history that keeps cropping up whenever there is an audience to wow. Working demonstrations of some of his work always have the audience transfixed, taking some minds back to the days of watching Flash Gordon on a black and white television. The name is: Nikola Tesla. How can his work still appear to be stuff of future science fiction - even after one hundred years? Is the world still not advanced enough to be able to take full advantage of some of his inventions?

Some of these ideas and inventions might be - and always be - unfulfilled or 'working with purpose' machines. Their only purpose - seems to be for now, is to look good in science shows! You could say, some of his work is rather akin to a time machine but within easier grasp to become some kind of reality?

Janus Alby was driving home from work on a spring evening, it was one of his last days at work before taking early retirement from his telecom research job. He was happy listening to the car radio whilst leaving the site of the research centre, as he always did on his journey home. This particular radio program was all about Tesla. Jan turned up the volume, *I used to love all this electrical high voltage coils and lightning stuff,* thought Jan as his mind began to slightly wander. *Maybe I should become a mad inventor, now that I'm nearly free! I'll get all the essential jobs around the house done, then I'm going to have a play all summer long. Hopefully, I can keep Chloe happy with a balance of - Yes, I can do that no problem! and when she's at work I can experiment. I'm nearly fifty-five so - perhaps I'm due for a bit of 'me' time!*

On retirement, Jan had originally planned to create a small home recording studio one day, with the aim of producing an album. He wasn't much of a musician; his style lay in producing electronic beats and samples. *Hmm, money could be a bit tight on my private pension,*

I'll have to see how things go and tread carefully when questioned.

On arrival home, Jan kissed his wife Chloe on the lips and held her thick dark shoulder length hair at the same time as he entered the front doorway.

'Did you have a good day,' she said. Jan said that he had and was starting to feel a bit nervous at the thought of retiring so early, did she think that it was still a good idea?

'It's the thought of losing a routine in your life I guess, don't worry I'll find you plenty to do,' she replied. H*mm - bummer,* thought Jan.

The following day was a Saturday, so it was odd-job time for Jan. He was a slightly nerdy type of chap; however, he was quite normal at the same time - but he still dressed a bit nerdy though! With a side parting to match. That morning he decided to clear out his large workshop, this had been a sanctuary for Jan in recent years, it was used for work and pleasure - he even toyed with the idea of moving in and selling the house at one point. He thought that as it had a decent pitched tiled roof and thick feather edge cladding, it would make a snug lodge.

He decided to still go with the dream of a recording studio - for now though. The workshop had become rather redundant of late and turned into a bit of a dumping ground. This was a bit of a shame as Jan had originally built the workshop to help him with his job and he had spent a lot of time and money on it. In the beginning, he was very proud of the workshop, which had become very useful, especially for doing extra work in the evenings. Mainly this extra work involved developing long distance communication networks - he was keen! Back then.

The workshop housed a cable testing rig and measurement facilities for optimising such networks, also, there were reels and drums of cable of all sizes. Jan decided to keep these for now as they were only borrowed in the first place and all-but forgot about by now. After some time, decluttering and making the workshop tidy, Jan had quite a few carloads of bits and pieces to take to the recycling centre. *First,* he thought, *I must return this circular saw back to Ivor on my way out. His constant asking for it back did become a platitude to me, it was over a year ago though!*

Later that day, on the way to the recycling centre, Jan stopped at Ivor's to hand back the saw. Ivor an old friend who was recently retired, only lived a few doors away from Jan, he knocked at the door, it was quickly answered by Ivor's wife Ellen.

'Oh. Hi Jan,' she said upon opening the door. She turned her head and shouted upstairs:

'Ivor, it's Jan, with your saw.' In reply there came a distant:

'J-Anus has finally decided to return it then.'
Jan shouted back:

'Remember I'm still taller than you!' He then left the saw on the step and quickly said bye, hopefully, avoiding a small dressing down from one of his closest friends, albeit a shorter one, with grey hair!

At the recycling centre Jan disposed of his rubbish and was about to sit into the driver's seat of his car when he noticed something. The man emptying the car in front of him was struggling with - what looked like some large wire mesh panels. *They could be handy for extra security for my workshop windows,* he thought. Stepping out of the car Jan approached the man.

'Excuse me, would you mind if I take them off your hands - if you are throwing them away that is?'

'Yeah, please take them,' came the reply.
Jan then loaded up the panels with the help of the man, and off he went. Back at home, he offloaded the mesh panels into his workshop, and stood them up in a corner. It was at this point he discovered that the panels all fitted together somehow. Eventually he worked out with a lot of huffing and puffing that together they formed a strong cube-shaped cage. *Was the chap who*

gave me the cage - some kind of zookeeper? Indeed, the cage 'was' big enough for an adult.

Jan carried on sorting out the workshop. After a while his wife Chloe came in with a cup of tea and some biscuits.

'I bet you would rather have a beer?' She said.

'Tell you what - I'll finish the tea and biscuits, then you can fetch me a beer!' He announced in reply.

'Anus,' was Chloe's reply to this, as she started to inspect the tidying up process in the workshop.

'Getting ready to fill the place out with expensive electronics? This of course, after you've done some essential jobs around the house,' quizzed Chloe.

'That's the idea. I might have to increase the security first though; I thought these mesh panels could be used for adding extra security in front of the windows.'

'All I can say is that you need to do a costing first, to see if we can actually afford to buy all the gear needed.'

'Will do! Sweetheart, now how about that beer,' Jan replied - smiling. With this, Chloe returned to the house.

Sometimes on a Saturday evening Jan and Ivor went out to the local pub called the 'The Two Bears' for a pint or two. This Saturday evening was one such visit.

'I've been thinking about a nice cold pint all day,' said Jan, this after a beer never materialised from Chloe in the workshop.

'Yeah, me too,' came Ivor's reply.

'How's the ephemeral studio coming on then Jan?' To this Jan replied that he had almost finished clearing it out, and the next task was to research and provide a costing for the equipment.

'Can't you find a cheaper hobby,' said Ivor. 'How about coming for a run with me, it's free you know!'

'Yeah, but running isn't really a 'bucket list' lifetime achievement kinda thing - is it? Anyway, you're always complaining that running gives you the stitch,' Jan added further.

'Yeah, I should really give up smoking, I guess,' came Ivor's reply.

Later, that week, Jan received a text from Ivor whilst he was at work. Ivor wanted to know if Jan fancied taking a jog with him that evening. After a while Jan texted back – *okay then, meet you at around seven outside your gate.* This was sent with some reluctance on Jan's behalf as the thought of 'going for a jog' didn't really appeal to him.

Later that day Jan, was approached by his manager, who asked if Jan would like to take some items back home with him before he retires.

'Remember that bespoke project we had a few months back, Jan?'

'What, the estuary cable?'

'Yes, that's right. You contributed a lot of work to that in your own time.'

'Yes, I did burn some midnight oil with that one,' replied Jan.

'Well, most of the stuff that you worked on is still in storage and you are welcome to take it with you, if you like? The high voltage copper coils might come in useful if you become a bit - work sick and want to have a play around or something. We can't turn them out to the field or re-purpose them here, it wouldn't be cost efficient!'

They then both went to the storage facility to inspect the items.

With Jan being the type of person not to 'look a gift horse in the mouth', he then loaded his car up. At leaving off time though, Jan had to drive home with extra diligence, due to the extra weight from the unexpected work haul...

It was just before Seven o'clock in the evening and Jan was waiting outside Ivor's gate. While he waited, he tried to keep some kind of jogging momentum going whilst also trying to keep a low profile from prying neighbours.

'To town via the park and back?' Said Ivor as he jogged up the short path to the gate.

Jan replied: 'Right you are. Steady though, as I haven't done this for years.'

So off they went. The urban circuit which they were following, was around three miles in total length. Ivor started off setting a good pace, which after a bit of time, Jan was struggling and puffing a bit to keep up.

'First one to the corner,' Ivor quickly shouted. They both raced and pounded along the pavement, in what seemed to them - in slow motion. Ivor inched ahead and by the time they had reached the corner, Jan had struggled to keep up the pace.

'Not bad for a man in his sixties,' said Ivor with a panting breath, following it up with:

'You know when I was a young man, I used to run for the county - that is, until I broke my leg.'

'Give me a bit more practice and I'll beat you, no problem,' puffed Jan.

'Mind you this stitch keeps coming and going, for some reason,' said Ivor, grimacing and bending over forward.

Jan thought that Ivor might be wise to spend a bit more time on warming up before engaging in exercise, but what did he know?

After a while on the return leg, Ivor suggested finishing up with a liquid warming down session in The Two Bears.

The Two Bears was the usual Victorian corner pub, dark green on the outside with white and orange detailing around the windows and door. It was quite small inside, many of the original fittings still remained - essentially the fireplace and bar! Not quite the 'Spit and sawdust' type, but a good-old regular. It even managed to serve some local ales and provided a basic food menu.

After a couple of pints Jan admitted that he did enjoy the run, and would like to do it more often.

'I'll start off with, a couple of times a week - if you'll have me,' said Jan. 'It might even help me to relieve the stress of early retirement.'

'Yes, I will be your mentor,' replied Ivor - rather - proficiently.

The following evening Jan started to seriously think about his home studio, so he set about doing some research and basic costing. *Well, the cost for just the basic setup runs into five figures. I can probably double that if I add in the cost for adapting the workshop...* Jan was starting to have doubts.

At bedtime Chloe quizzed Jan about his findings. He had to admit that setting up a studio was probably going to be a bit too expensive, and he might have to have a bit of a rethink.

'I could buy some of the larger things secondhand,' said Jan, with a slight feeling of despondency starting to quietly creep in. Chloe replied cheerfully:

'That's risky, but never mind, you can have a go at cleaning the gutters and windows this weekend. Call it - a gentle start to a summer of odd jobs. Maybe you could find something less costly to do in your workshop? What about all that cable and all the wires that you brought home from work, isn't there something that you could do with them?'

'Maybe,' replied Jan.

The following week was Jan's last week at work. There wasn't much chance of any real work to be done, especially at home – in the evening time. With this in mind Jan decided to arrange a couple of evening runs with Ivor.

As before, Jan and Ivor jogged the usual route and they decided to finish off in the Two Bears pub.

After chatting for a while Ivor asked Jan how his last week was going and had he made any decisions about his studio.

'My last week mainly consists of buying cakes and tidying up. The studio might have to wait until I win the Lotto.'

To this Ivor asked if all the cable and test gear could, maybe be of any use.

'Well, Ivor, as all that stuff didn't cost anything - I might tinker around with it.'

They finished up and agreed to go for another run later that week.

The next day at work Jan was chatting to Charlie, his work colleague. The two discussed what Jan had planned for early retirement and about the donation of estuary job items from their line manager. Charlie explained to Jan that he had only just found out that the coils were quite special and expensive, apparently the coils were highly conductive, and highly efficient, due to their high silver content. Company policy would normally be that due to their value they should have really been sold for scrap, but it was a nice parting gift anyway. He did admit to Jan that he would have also liked to have the coils to experiment with. Charlie also remarked that if Jan wanted some help with any of his projects sometime in the future, he would like to lend a hand.

Charlie lived on his own, he was very similar in his appearance and personality to Jan. The main difference between them though was that Charlie was your archetypal nerd; Oxbridge educated and very clever. However, he was single and living alone, so he was always on the lookout for a chance of more socialising - especially with friends. Jan promised that if he got round to it, he would ask for his help, as Charlie - was the brains of the two!

That evening, Jan started to do some online research into Tesla and his inventions, after remembering hearing the radio documentary recently on his way home from work. As he already had the 'free' cable and wound technology, it would make sense to try and do something with them - even if he had to throw them all away, it would still be at no cost to him. Jan came to the conclusion that the coils he had from work, could possibly be used in making some sort of prototype.

Friday came. Jan's last day at work.

'Retire from your job, but never retire your mind.' This came echoing down the corridor from Jan's manager - very short in stature, but very tall audibly, as they approached each other.

'I'm not planning to rest that, just yet' Jan stated.

'Well, if you ever get bored or want any help with anything, let me know. You never know, you might want a part time job later on?'

'I will keep my options open,' said Jan, as he proceeded to find Charlie. After finding Charlie, Jan explained that he might have a go at trying to do one of Tesla's experiments, what did Charlie think of that?

'Well, if you want, I can do some research to see how much work is involved. I'm sure though, that you are halfway there, especially as you already have a lot of the parts - like the coils and your test rig.'

Jan then thanked Charlie who promised to update him sometime later on in the next week.

That evening Jan and Ivor went for another run, finishing off in the pub again. Ivor gulped down his first drink of ale, announcing while spitting out some froth:

'The first one - and the best one. Cheers, then. Well, now that you are retired - like me. What have you got planned for this weekend then Jan?'

'I've decided to put the studio on hold for now, as I might have to get a part time job to fund it. It's with utmost importance that utopia prevails back at the castle.'

'So, what are you going to do then Jan.'

'Amongst doing the obligatory odd jobs around the house, I've decided to have a play around with the cable and stuff that we chatted about. Have you heard of someone called Nikola Tesla?'

'Yes, of course. He's the guy who invented that coil with all that sparking electricity which could have come out of Frankenstein's laboratory, isn't he?'

'Yes. I'm going to have a go at creating my own coil - I think? I'm pretty sure that I have a lot of the parts that are needed.'

Ivor surprised Jan by saying:

'I saw a programme about him a while back, some guys were messing around with these big wire coils and a LOT of high voltage electricity. Sparks everywhere. I've seen this before, but these guys were also trying to incorporate some sort of enclosed box or cage. I don't know what it was made of, or the purpose for it. It made me laugh though, because if they entered the cage with the power on it made them feel dizzy almost immediately. A couple of them were almost sick as well. I can't really remember much more as I thought that they were a bit crazy, and I wasn't paying too much attention anyway.'

It was Jan's round, he collected the glasses and headed towards the bar, thinking on the way about what Ivor had said. *That's kinda weird - what was the point of those guy's building a cage?*

'Work is the curse of the drinking classes - according to Oscar Wilde,' Jan recited in a thespian-like voice on his arrival back at the table.

'Paranormal, ghosts and such like!' Ivor exclaimed in reply. 'That's what the idea of the cage was for. They thought that the energy from the coils could attract spirits, ghosts or whatever?' Jan still stood at the table - Ivor carried on:

'It must have been one of those ghost hunting shows that I saw the experiment on.' Jan sat down and replied:

'Well, I guess that adds another dimension to it for me to play around with. I'm not sure that I believe in life after death or is it: death after life?'

They finished up their drinks and headed back, deciding that the next week they could try and go for a run during the day, but probably not go to the pub.

Chapter Two

That weekend was wet, the wind was playing through the fence panels and trees like a continuous and extended musical discord. Chloe had some outside jobs lined up for Jan, but these were put on hold due to the inclement weather. This did mean, however, that Jan had the opportunity to play around in his workshop.

He lifted the coils out of their boxes, forgetting about how well they had been engineered - they had all probably been handmade. Each one stood around half a metre tall, and he had a dozen of them in number, and doubtless, very expensive to manufacture! Jan thought it was best to experiment with just one coil at first.

These coils won't spark up on their own, they will require some kind of primary coil to drive them. Hopefully, I'll be able to repurpose some of the cable that I already have.

After a while Jan had arranged some cable in the shape of a horizontal Catherine wheel to form a primary coil. The purpose of this was to induce current into the tightly wound secondary coil. The cable test rig that was already in-situ in the workshop wasn't really suitable for this kind of experiment. However, it could produce a high voltage burst, which might be of use for his experiment, initially.

Later after much fiddling and hmm-ing and urrr-ing, Jan was ready to fire up the test rig. Hopefully, this would inject a burst of energy into the makeshift coil assembly. Setting the rig to max output voltage, with a timed rapid burst output, he stood back and counted down to himself: *five, four, three, two, one, and...* The test rig hummed and vibrated under the intense energy it had to produce, the coils, however, were still and lifeless. Then, a spark leapt from the conductor at top of the tall coil and 'cracked' through the still silent air. It leapt straight to a close-by metal power socket on the workshop wall - then on down to the earth.

Jan couldn't break his concentration from looking at the spot where the spark had just momentarily been. His mind was immediately taken back to the time when he was a young lad, walking and playing in the local woods. After playing, he sometimes slumped down against a tree in order to catch his breath, this of course, after 'another' downing of 'yet' more stormtroopers on their speedster bikes. Sometimes - for a change though, he would make a world record jump on his bike across a make-believe chasm.

Whilst sitting down, he would become encapsulated, staring up at the giants with their multiple branches, which - to him, looked like they were conducting the gentle wind. In doing so, channeling this invisible mighty force through a highly organised and ushered linear route - to quickly exit it through the woods, then on to wrap around the first human in its path. There was more to see though - for Jan. At these times when the contrast of light and dark in the woods were at just the right balance, what his eyes could see, and his mind could process was a – magic-like energy. This was tipped with blues and light greens and dancing at low levels from almost every living thing - physical or plant around him. His eyes locked in a stare, a bit like crossing them and mildly panicking when they won't straighten very quickly when you want to see straight again.

This 'special' power of seeing into another world - as Jan put it to his friends, would normally be something that would scare him, making him think that there was something wrong with his eyes. However, he kind of knew that it wasn't anything to question or be of concern about.

As he grew older, his witnessing of auras became less frequent, and more-or-less forgotten.

I haven't seen anything like that since I was a boy, he thought to himself, whilst still staring at the coil. *That reality of the crisp spark and audible crack it made in the air - like a memory trigger!* Soon after, Chloe came in.

'Stand against the wall.'

'You what,' she replied.

'I just want to look at you against the wall.'

'Have you gone mad? - oh, all right then.' After a couple of minutes of Jan staring at Chloe he said softly:

'Yep, I can still see it - faintly.'

'What on earth are you talking about?'
Chloe was now starting to get a bit impatient.

'You didn't know that I had a gift for seeing auras, did you?'

'You've never mentioned it - what does mine look like then?'

'I can't see it completely; I can only see the aura standing out for a few inches from your body outline. It's like a white mini electric field, dancing away from your body surface.'

'Well, it's good to know that I still have some energy left in me!' They both then headed indoors for some lunch.

Do you fancy going for a jog on Monday - your first day of freedom? Say, at seven in the morning - pinged a text (from Ivor) on Jan's phone during his lunch break. *Yep. Meet you at the usual place!* Jan texted back in reply.

Later back in the workshop, Jan made up a few more coil assemblies. Each one more-or-less reacted in the same way as the first one when they were energised from the test rig. Jan knew that to progress his experiment he had to modify the existing coils and purchase some other parts, if he really wanted to turn them into something breathtaking - that is?

As a treat for both of them that afternoon, Jan decided to take Chloe out for dinner to a local restaurant. It used to be a regular haunt for them, but they hadn't visited very much in the past few years as they were seldom at home long enough together.

A particular favourite dish for Jan was Niçoise Beef. He noticed that it was still on the menu, but the last time he had the dish, it was nearly his last meal… Halfway through the beef, Jan managed to get a piece of - let's say: not fully chewed beef stuck in his throat, it was only cleared after the intervention of another diner. It wasn't life threatening as such, but it required some firm back slapping to dislodge it.

'I do really fancy the Niçoise Beef.'

'No, you don't. I thought that you were going to die last time you had it, when you nearly choked,' came a stern reply from Chloe.

'Yeah, I was quite scared. At the time, it all seemed to be in slow motion and as if I were looking down on myself. You're right - I'll have the curry instead.'

It was the following day, at around seven in the morning. Jan met Ivor at his gate, they then set about jogging their usual route.

'Shall we up the pace a bit then Jan?'

'Yes, okay, I think I could up my game a bit.'

They kept up a steady pace through the park, to which Jan was keeping abreast of Ivor. Once out of the park gate they had to cross the high street, stopping as there was more traffic than normal, it was a busy weekday with many cars en route to work and school.

'After this red car, then,' said Ivor, gripping his side.

'You got the stitch again Ivor?'

'Yeah, but it's not too bad for now.'

They carried on - still at a good pace, until they had to cross the same road again to start the return leg home. By this time, Ivor was struggling a bit more and asked Jan if they could stop for a second, to see if the pain from the stitch would ease.

'Yes, no problem, we'll have to wait to cross again anyway, take a second Ivor.'

Ivor stopped and lent forward to try and ease the pain
- in doing so, he took an impetuous step off the kerb -
then time seemed to slow down for Jan…

'NO!' Shouted Jan - it was too late! Ivor had already
been struck by a fast-moving car; now braking very
hard! It was still moving fast enough for Ivor to go over
top of it though!

To Jan, this all happened in slow motion and did
bizarrely remind him of an angry bull in a bullfight,
trying to toss the Matador's cape over its head.

'Keep still Ivor, I'll call for help!' Said Jan as he ran
to the spot in the road where Ivor had landed - like a
doll tossed from a rooftop. People started to gather
around, there was little response from Ivor. Jan was
shaking and stumbling to get his words out on his phone
to the emergency services, but at the same time, rushing
to tell them the details.

A man from the gathering crowd had already placed
his coat over Ivor and he was also checking Ivor's
pulse.

'Pulse seems okay, I'm no doctor though. You've
just called for an Ambulance - haven't you?'

'Yes,' replied Jan.

After a couple of minutes, the emergency services
arrived. They quickly administered first aid and carried
out some checks on Ivor before loading him into the

ambulance. The police were also on the scene, questioning Jan and trying to establish what had actually happened. *My mind has gone blank and I'm shaking like a leaf, why can't I even work out how to call Chloe?*

'Chloe, it's me. This is bad! I'm on the high street, Ivor has been involved in an accident with a car. I'm not sure how bad he is, he's just been taken to hospital in the ambulance, and I'll be there as soon as the Police have finished questioning me. Please call Ellen and take her to A&E.'

At the hospital, Jan met up with Chloe and Ivor's wife Ellen. The doctor was already giving an update to Ellen, she was crying.

'This is surely all a dream Chloe.'

'Whatever happened,' replied Chloe. Jan went on to explain what had happened.

'There's nothing that you could have done. It sounded as if it was a total accident,' Chloe said, trying to make Jan see that it was all probably unintentional. Jan excused himself and headed into the toilet, his mind was going into overdrive, self-perpetuating - making him feel slightly nauseous…

Fate will be decided - not on YOUR thoughts and self-muttering prayers. You will descend - for now, into the pit of self-pity and hopelessness and be tortured by your very thoughts. Those convoluted thoughts - digging into your every waking moment. The second that you start to think anything - I will be there gratuitously - to challenge and test your equanimity.

The three of them spent the rest of the day waiting at the hospital. Finally, just before midnight, one of the accident and emergency doctors emerged to report on Ivor's condition.

'He's stable for now - which is good! He's still unconscious, which is to be expected as he's suffered quite a bit of bruising.' The doctor then went on to recommend that they all go home and get some rest. Chloe decided to stay with Ellen for the night, in case there was any change with Ivor, and they needed to quickly get to the hospital. At home, Jan knew that it was pretty hopeless going to bed and trying to get some sleep. He decided to go into his workshop and carry on with his experiments - if only to try and curtail his inner thoughts.

As Jan had partially succeeded in generating a spark with the first coil, he decided to double up on the number of coils this time. A few hours later, Jan had set up another working coil, testing it by itself first, then together with the first coil. The two coils both produced a similar spark. Jan knew that he needed to fine tune the coils and find a better way to drive them properly through experimentation to eventually achieve the results for which he was aiming for. After a few hours, tiredness got the better of Jan, so he retired back to the house - then to bed.

Early the next day, Ellen called the hospital for an update on Ivor. The hospital reported that he was still unconscious, but stable. Chloe said that she and Ellen would go to visit Ivor, as the police will probably want to speak to Jan at some point during the day. Sure enough, at around 10 o'clock there came a knock at the door from the police. Jan was questioned intensely about the previous day's events, until the police were satisfied with Jan's version. Before they left, the constable did also state that several witnesses had already come forward, and that all had witnessed events that colluded with Jan's version of what had happened.

After Jan had some lunch, he made his way to the hospital to meet up with Chloe.

'Ivor's still about the same, although he has made a few small movements according to the nurse,' explained Chloe as Jan approached her when he entered the waiting room.

'Ellen is in there with him now.'

Jan and Chloe waited around, and after a few hours they both got the opportunity to go in and see Ivor, then in the early evening they returned home. After a while, Jan decided to catch up on some emails, which amongst overs that were in his inbox, was a message from Charlie:

Hi Jan. How are you? An update on my findings about the Tesla Coils. I'm guessing that you have already managed to get at least one of the coils to do something? My findings mainly concern your test rig that you have in your workshop. From what I can find "You're in luck" I've found what they call a "Resonant transformer module" for sale online. It just slips into the expansion module rack on your rig, plus it's not very expensive! I've included the link at the end. Also, you probably know this, but you might have to spend a bit of time tuning the device and also fit some kind of Toroid at the top of the secondary coil.

Jan immediately clicked on the link that Charlie had included in the message. *Charlie is right, I'll order the module straightaway.* With a click, it was all paid for.

The following day they all visited Ivor again at the hospital. Ivor was showing further signs of progress, but he was still unconscious. The next few days followed a similar pattern, with all three of them spending much of the day at the hospital. A doctor at the hospital did state that the type of injuries Ivor had sustained in the accident were common - for that type of collision. They were also quite confident that much of the bruising would ease quite quickly. The main concern was the injury that Ivor sustained to his head from probably hitting the windscreen, and also the impact from hitting his head on the road when he landed. However, after about a week the doctors were confident that this head injury was slightly improving, Ivor had even started to come around - to everyone's relief!

'How are you feeling old man?' Were Jan's first words to Ivor.

'I've felt better, thanks.'

'It's great to see that you have come around and appear to be still in working order.'

'Well, I'm still here, but I don't know if I'm still in full working order though? I don't really know anything much - they tell me that I went over the top of a car. Is that what you saw Jan?'

'Yes, I saw it alright! I think you lost your balance - or something, when you got the stitch again.'

'I can't remember a thing.' Replied Ivor.
With a slightly sombre tone, Jan asked:

'Seriously though, I thought that you had been killed.'

'It was all just black to me; I had no perception of consciousness until I recently woke up - zilch.'

'Well, it's great, to have you back Ivor.'
The two of them carried on chatting for a little while longer about the times that they have had together. This was until a nurse came in and said that Jan should let Ivor rest for a while.

'I'll pop in to see you tomorrow then Ivor.'

'Make it in the evening please, as I have Ellen coming back this afternoon. I'm guessing that I'll be pretty exhausted tomorrow morning, with all today's activity, and probably will need to rest until the afternoon.'

'OK, see you tomorrow evening then!'
As Jan exited the door, Ivor quickly said:

'Anyhow, if I did go, you could have probably got in touch with me, with your coil thing?'

'Ha - yeah. That's one experiment that I gladly won't need to try out now.'

On his arrival home, Jan updated Chloe on Ivor's progress. They both agreed about how relieved they were now that Ivor has finally come around, and that he now, seems to be getting back to normal.

'Oh, by the way, a parcel arrived for you today Jan. It's quite a big box, I've placed it in the study for you.'

'Thanks, Clo - nice one.'

That's brilliant! Now that we're rest assured that Ivor is on the mend, perhaps I can spend a bit more time playing around with my setup. Jan sat down for his dinner, which he quickly devoured so that he could spend some quality time in his workshop.

In his workshop Jan looked at his parcel, which he already knew was the module for the cable test rig. He opened it up, unwrapped it and checked to make sure that it would indeed fit the rig. However, he decided that he would wait until everything else was in place before he would switch on the rig. Waiting, and wanting to make sure that he had all the other parts in place before the grand switch on. Jan's attention then turned towards how he was going to find a Toroid or Torus, the doughnut shaped part that sits at the top of the coil and spits out all the mini lightning. This was a more problematic part for Jan to source as the coils were a 'one off' so a toroid that would fit - could be a more difficult part to find. After some searching online, Jan decided on the most cost effective, and efficient way, to construct his toroid. His method would be to use a small diameter aluminium pipe formed into a coil, then formed to make a torus shape. So, within a little while some pipe was ordered online that fitted the criteria.

A couple of days later, the pipe arrived. Jan immediately set to work, forming, and shaping with adroit hands. This all borne out of the utmost determination not to kink the pipe, as it was quite expensive. You see, Jan was a very prudent person - with money - that is! He spent the best part of the day fine tuning and fixing the spring like doughnut to the coil. Finally at the end of the day - and feeling quite pleased with himself, he decided to have a grand switch on - the following day.

Early afternoon, the following day, Jan was ready for the switch on. He powered up the test rig, which was now fitted with the module. Then he stood back, trembling with anticipation, and trying to prepare himself for the airborne static charge about to be inflicted on his body. Well, that didn't happen! There were some sparks from the coil, which were about the same as last time. This of course - before Jan had spent lots of time and money on it!

Chapter Three

The lightning awoke Jan - he quickly sat up. The flashes were so bright - even in full daylight.

'What's the time?'

'Half-six Jan.'

'I said that I would go and visit Ivor this morning. I'll get soaked if this storm hasn't moved on.'

'Well, he is expecting you! Be a brave boy Jan!'

'Bloody vociferous thunderstorms,' muttered Jan as he turned back over.

By the time Jan left to visit Ivor, the storm had in fact - gotten worse!

'How are you today then Ivor?'

'I'm quite drained today, probably because I'm bored, and I had a full day of visits yesterday.'
After hearing this, Jan persuaded Ivor to remain in bed whilst they chatted.

'You know there is a school of philosophy who believes that just being in hospital can trick the mind in some people. This then, can make them think that they are ill, or more ill - than they actually are?'

'I totally agree,' replied Ivor, nodding his head. 'I can't wait to get out of here, it must be soon! At this moment, however, - I just need to get some rest.'
Ivor was struggling to keep his eyes open, so Jan quietly left the room and headed home.

Once home, Chloe asked Jan how Ivor was doing.

'He's exhausted, so-much-so, he could hardly keep awake. I left him to get some rest. Didn't even say bye to him!'

'He will feel a lot better for a good day's rest, I think,' said Chloe, reassuringly.

Over the next couple of days, Jan tinkered around with his experiment. Slowly, but surely, he was increasing the strength of the coil output, creating a more powerful spark through tuning the coil with signalling, and then measuring the output. By the end of a couple of day's tinkering, he was getting quite an impressive light show, as well as a loud crack of static in the air. This had got to the point of giving Jan the feeling that his hair was standing on end.

Later that evening and feeling rather pleased with himself, Jan opened up a bottle of wine and poured out a glass for Chloe and himself.

'I take it that you are progressing with your coil experiment thingy, Jan?'

'Yes, I feel like I'm really getting somewhere with it now.'

'At least you aren't sitting around - I guess. If you were - that would drive me nuts!' Said Chloe, ending the sentence with a slightly sterner tone of voice.

'You know that I'm not one for sitting around Chloe. Before you know, I'll be onto something else that might have some monetary income value to it!'

After another glass or two, they both relaxed more and started to discuss what the future might hold for them. They couldn't agree on too much, but they both agreed that they would like to spend more time together.

Now. Drinking tends to make time speed up - for some inexplicable reason? Before they knew it, the clock's arms were fully raised - like it was about to take a plunge into a swimming pool. Noticing this, they thought it was time that they settled down. So off they went to bed, slightly drunk and very tired...

In bed, it quickly became very dark for Jan. The next thing he knew was that he was floating around the countryside in brilliant sunshine, with some of his old workmates. For some reason they were all continuously falling down deep holes - but somehow, ending back where they all started? All of a sudden! - Back in the real world, the telephone began ringing...

'Can you get that Jan?'

Coming out of his dreamworld, Jan didn't know where on earth he was - or what he was doing. After all, he'd only been asleep for about an hour!

'Jan.'

Said the voice on the other end of the line, after a second or two of silence.

'I shouldn't have called but I have some really bad news.'

Jan immediately knew exactly what was coming next, as the caller was Ellen...

This is the point that your heart leaps up into your mouth, your throat develops a lump, and you gasp for water. You feel like a kid again all anxious and nervous - fighting to stop your voice from hiding somewhere in the pits of your stomach. Words were difficult for Ellen from here.

'It's about Ivor, Isn't it Ellen?'

Ellen then burst into tears.

'I think it's best that we come over to you Ellen.'

After spending the rest of the night comforting Ellen, Chloe and Jan needed to catch up on some sleep themselves, and to also to start taking-in the death of Ivor. Respite came with the arrival of Ivor and Ellen's two grown-up children, who had been travelling through the night.

On the way back home, Jan and Chloe didn't really say anything to each other. Trance like, they headed straight to bed, and somehow, fell asleep.

'I just can't believe that he's gone, croaked Jan, upon waking up and seeing that Chloe was already awake. She replied:

'The doctors think that the cause was a sudden bleed to the brain. As Ivor was showing good progress, he was taken off some of the monitoring equipment. I guess - that's the risk, maybe he should have been more closely monitored for longer? Unfortunately, it all happened whilst he was asleep, there was no one there for him at that particular time. It could all be over in a short period of time in that situation.'

'Hopefully, there will be some sort of enquiry as to what 'exactly' happened,' Jan finished.

'Let's hope so,' said Chloe.

'All we can do for now, is give our support to Ellen.'

The next few days were emotional and busy for all concerned. The coroner confirmed the cause of death, so that the family could arrange the funeral. Ellen asked Chloe and Jan if they wouldn't mind contacting Ivor's closest friends and arranging some kind of wake. Jan chose to have a spread in the Two Bears pub - it seemed fitting, as it was their local watering hole.

'It's bloody weird, this life thing Clo!'

'What do you mean,' she replied as they sat down for an evening meal.

'Well, this week - now for instance, we are sitting down for a meal... Next week, it could be me being nailed into my wooden box?'

'It could be, but nothing has changed there, as there's always that threat - for everybody. It's at times like these, that we all question our mortality, it's never far away. Usually, we don't tend to think about it so much.'

'Where is he now? What I mean is: does everything just go back into the ether? All those memories, emotions, ideas, and love? Is it the end of everything, or is life just a word for being here, in this dimension? Do you move on, like moving to a new house without looking back to the old one? Like walking out of school on your last day. Is it - really that exciting for every passing? So much so, that nobody ever wants to come back to the physical body? Perhaps once you realise what's beyond, you just wouldn't want to return and be bound by the limitation of skin and bone, again, imprisoned and fixed to the earth's soil and rock for the full term. I wonder what level the physical world is located on, in the tower block of all dimensions?'

'Maybe, you can work that one out, in your workshop one day? We have things to do at the moment - hopefully with a certain amount of equanimity.'

On the day of the funeral, the weather was miserable, rain lashing down and quite windy. The service itself was the usual affair. Ivor's eulogy, as read by the celebrant, was pieced together like an audible comic book of eclectic, semi-idiosyncratic events. This is of course - as usual, when there is a sudden death, writing down everybody else's version of the said moments. Time doesn't allow for any checks as to whether their thoughts were loyal to what actually happened or not! Hopefully, Ivor told the truth about the standout things that he did by himself. Either way it doesn't really matter; it's probably better to say that you sprinted up a mountain and fell off halfway down. This rather than tell the truth, that you needed a supply of oxygen after two hundred metres going up, and a helicopter to get down...

'Thank you ever-so much for helping me out. I don't think that I could have got through this without you two.' This was the first thing that Ellen said to Chloe and Jan as they entered the door of the Two Bears. It was spoken in a calm and almost uplifting way - as if a weight had been slightly lifted from Ellen's shoulders.

Curly-headed Ellen seemed a touch more vibrant - especially now that all of her locks had been - 're-sprung'. She had always been slight in build and very lightweight, however, she could pack a punch! Probably, somewhat of a 'dark horse'.

At times! Closure can tend to offer an air of calmness and coming together - maybe a start of a new chapter (although unwanted for most) thought Jan to himself.

They did the rounds, chatting and offering some solace at times. After a while, Chloe and Jan did finally manage to sit down and have a bite to eat. On filling his mouth with food, Jan made a comment:

'Not bad these sandwiches, good old favourites, I'm sure Ivor would have enjoyed them. Especially with a pint.'

'Ha.'

'Sorry?' Jan said.

Chloe replied:

'I don't know what you're going on about Jan? I couldn't understand what you were saying, and I wasn't really listening. I certainly didn't say anything back!'

'I'm sure that someone laughed, I thought that it was you, Chloe?' I must be hearing things then, after all it's been a weird couple of weeks, probably time to fetch another pint!'

After a while Ellen came over to the table. She'd had enough and was drained with all what had happened, and all the emotion that came with it.

Jan returned from the bar with the drinks. He stopped quickly though, as soon as he saw Ellen sitting with Chloe. For some reason he could see a bright aura surrounding Ellen. This was more vivid than any that he had seen as a child, this unsettled Jan a bit, as he normally would have to go into a semi relaxed state of concentration to see - even the beginnings of an aura field. Jan then turned his attention to somebody entering the door, he looked back again at Ellen, the aura had gone.

Once they had got home and settled down, Jan mentioned to Chloe about the aura. She didn't seem overly interested though, saying something about Jan overthinking things and probably having too much to drink! They both then quickly fell to sleep.

Those who walk and breathe on the earth, shall never have the right to gain knowledge of other worlds within the realm of the universes. You shall not be able to properly see or comprehend any other world, than the world that you are bound to... Minds are locked within their realm, and duty bound to only serve as an aid to propagate the same. The physical mind does not have the ability to understand and nurture itself of other dimensions.

'Wow! How weird was that dream,' Jan muttered to himself upon waking up the next morning.

As this was the first time that Jan had any time for himself in a few days, he decided to catch up on a few jobs. He even thought that he might be able to spend some time in the 'Lab' - as he now called the workshop. He hoped that by renaming the workshop it would give his experiment more of a deep cultured, nineteenth century air of mystery...

Eventually, well into the evening time by now, Jan managed to get into the lab. *All this seems as if it has all changed now. It all feels different! What do I do now, should I scrap this stupid idea and get myself a part time job? That would be 'really' sensible, Chloe would love that. This somehow feels deeper now, as if I have a duty to see this thing through. Something - deep down, is pulling me to carry on, could it be that I need to connect? - To what?*

Jan started to go through with what he had already done so far - like a recap. Looking through all his parts, he came across the cage that he acquired from the local recycling centre. Looking at it and thinking about what Ivor had said about the programme that he had seen on television. *Is there something in that television programme that Ivor was telling me about? Is this experiment about to take a weird twist?*

Jan decided to get some advice from his mate Charlie, as he had already promised Jan some help. Jan set about composing an email to mainly ask Charlie about his thoughts on using the cage as part of his experiment.

Later the following day, Jan's phone pinged with a text reply from Charlie:

Hi Jan. I haven't ever seen a sealed enclosure used in this sort of way before. Although anything is possible - I guess? I'm thinking that you would have to reduce the size of the cage to maximise efficiency, and probably use all the coils to feed the area evenly?!? Let me know how you get on.

So, over the next couple of days, Jan sourced and ordered all the necessary parts to help him make up the remaining ten coils. Once all the parts had arrived, he knew that it was going to take him at least a couple of weeks to get all of the coils working together.

So, after a few weeks, Jan had arranged what looked like something out of Doctor Who, on the floor of his Lab. He was kind of stuck now. He knew how to carry on, and what his goal might be, but the problem was in the implementation of the experiment. He thought that it was about time that he invited Charlie over!

'Wow, Jan, that's some kind of setup! Does It power up?'

'Oh yes Charlie, I'll show you.'
Jan flicked the switch, the test rig created a deep humming sound and vibrated, intensely. It struggled to keep up with the power demands of all twelve coils. It was indeed - a spectacular display of dancing mini-lightning bolts, all cracking in the air at random times.

'So, what about this enclosure then Jan?'

'My method of thinking has slightly changed, what with recent events, and all that.'

'Yes, I'm sorry to hear about what happened to your friend Jan.'

'You know, it's strange how a tragic event can change your skew on everything, I guess most of it is temporary, but I'm told, we all learn a little from everything, everyday.'

Jan dug out the cage and struggled, with the help of Charlie, to set it up.

'Well, you're certainly going to have to cut it down, overwise you might need a power station to charge the air up in this monster!'

'What do you suggest?'

'I don't know, maybe there should be just enough room for you, whilst sitting on a chair?'

They carried on talking it through, and they finally decided on the dimensions of the enclosure. Charlie also discussed possible ways to charge the cage from the coils. Much of this was theoretical of course, as not much research had been done - that was public knowledge anyway.

It took Jan a couple more weeks of cutting and shaping the cage, to get it just right. Jan also had to electrically bond all of the enclosure, apart from, part of the floor - on Charlie's advice, of course!

So finally, it was time to try out this weird experiment. Jan completed all the checks and had his hand hovering on the power switch – then, Ping! He received a text message on his phone:

Make sure that you fit a wired panic button to kill the power on your rig. Keep it with you at all times inside the enclosure!! Take care! Charlie.

Hmm - wise man, - thought Jan.

Chapter Four

Hello Charlie, I've set it all up like we discussed, powered it up and there is 'some' action, and a bit of fireworks. That's about it though, to be honest - I'm a bit at a loss. I'm not even sure what should happen next?

- MESSAGE SENT

Jan didn't mention to Charlie about how engrossed he had started to become about the whole idea though. In pursuit of obtaining the best results for himself, when he was in the cage, Jan had ditched his usual jacket and jeans in favour of a tee shirt and shorts. He even had his hair shaved to about half an inch, so that there was even less of an obstacle between his brain and - whatever was going to happen in the cage!

Later, Jan and Charlie talked through the possible cause, to try and explain the under performance of the experiment. The only thing that they could agree to do next, was to carry out yet more research...

A couple of days later, it was lunchtime and Jan was starving! Chloe was at her part time job, so Jan was on his own. Looking through the fridge, Jan could hear Chloe's voice in his head saying: *Maybe you can have this leftover jacket potato tomorrow for lunch?* He got it out, and placed it straight into the microwave. He hit the reheat button and carried on with preparing his lunch. A few seconds later he started to smell burning. He turned to look at the microwave, there was a small amount of sparking, and some smoke was filtering out through the door seal. *That'll be the foil that I forgot to remove from the spud then!* There was no damage done, and the potato was still edible! He paused to think about what had just happened. *Hmm, that's given me an idea.*

Later on, while speaking to Charlie on the phone, Jan explained what had happened, and if the idea of a foil like conductor within the cage could excite and enhance the space within to produce some results. Charlie said it could be an idea, however, ordinary foil might be a bit too crude, he'll do some more research.

In bed that night, Jan was doing some research on his laptop, Chloe was just about asleep. She started to breathe more slowly and deeply as she slipped into a deep sleep. It was a fairly warm night so there was only a thin sheet covering Chloe. Jan sat up and took note as the sheet rose up and down with Chloe's breathing. He thought: *Maybe I'm missing something here? If we can get more in tune with Mother nature's law of dynamics, it's just possible that it might help us go beyond what we can see. We have power at the minute, but little control! Even lightning strikes go up as well as down.* Jan was now starting to understand what was required to carry his experiment forward. The answer was partly in the past - as always! He just had to relax, clear his mind and almost meditate and let the answers come to him, as he did when he was a kid whilst seeing auras.

We are all as one, working in tandem with everything in the World - Universe, even! Our hearts beat with the ticking of time, the ebb and flow of the tides juxtaposed with night and day. Maybe all the answers - to everything, were created at the same time as the Universe was? Forever forbidden to be taken off the shelf like a book, for a quick answer - maybe? Perhaps the destiny of everything - ever, is just sitting there - like in a natural cyberspace, in the dark matter or something? Even if we could access it, I guess we would still be at the mercy of interpreting all of this information - God help us!

He then fell asleep.

Later, Jan decided to make the Lab more accommodating, so a wood burning stove was ordered. He hoped this would be able to extend the time he could spend there on the colder evenings, later on in the year. He didn't quite go as far as fitting curtains, but he did fit some heavy duty black out blinds, and a solid door. He didn't really want the neighbours to start suspecting anything, as the lab would probably be lighting up like a 'Christmas tree' in the darker evening times.

Back to his experiment, he decided to make a semi start again, with the coils. Going with the thoughts of the previous night, he decided to disconnect all of the coils from the test rig. He also made up a crude switching overlapping relay circuit, which would continuously power up and down only half of the number of coils at any one time. Jan needed to perfect the circuit so that it would allow for a variable power overlap for each bank of coils. *This is where Charlie could help,* he thought. Before Jan had the chance to message Charlie, he received an email from - Charlie:

Hi Jan. I've done some research and had some thoughts about what we discussed the other day. I've discovered something they call Graphene; it comes as a sheet material. Apparently, they call it a 'wonder material' and it's going to revolutionise electronics as

*we know it. It has many properties - so there's no harm
in trying it as a regulator within the cage - maybe?*
The message carried on with what Charlie thought
would be the best area to place the sheets and how much
to use. Also, the use of an arrestor system to ground the
sheets - if it all became a bit overpowering!

Jan and Charlie continued to exchange messages
over the following few days with ideas and suggestions.
Eventually, Jan had ended up with quite a long
shopping list of parts to obtain.

After a week or so, most of the ordered parts had
been delivered. Jan made sure that he had the next
couple of days free, so that he could crack on.

The time came at last, for another switch on. Jan had
also obtained a couple of peripheral cards for the test
rig to even out and boost the power available. He had
yet to fit many of the parts, as he thought that building
the experiment up, a small bit at a time, would lessen
the chances of any future problems.

Starting with the coil banks, He powered them up
and 'low and behold' they popped and fizzed with the
rhythmic timing of the new switch-over circuit. Jan
looked at the seat in the cage, thinking to himself,
whether he dared to finally sit inside it, or not? He
slowly moved towards it, entering into it very slowly,
and clutching the kill switch, he sat down. He didn't

experience anything for a few seconds. Then all of a sudden, he started to feel lightheaded - like the kind of feeling that you get when you lie down still after a few drinks, but the light fitting above your head keeps on moving. He gave it a few more seconds, then - bang, he hit the panic button! *Wow! That's certainly doing something! I don't know what to make of it though. It kinda scares me, but I want to try it again.* His method of thinking was that if he got used to being in that kind of environment, he would eventually start to get used to it?

Over the next couple of days, he tried it a couple of more times, but it had the same effect every time. He thought that it could really be the end of the whole experiment, as he had created something that he physically couldn't withstand.

Jan decided to persevere with the job in hand and to try and fit the Graphene sheets. Now! - Both Charlie and Jan decided that the sheets might be best placed on the chair, this was so that the energy could partly filter itself through Jan. Jan decided, however, that the sheets would play a better role if they were on the sides of the cage, for safety and effectiveness.

After some time: *Right all the sheets are fitted - let's try again!* The power was surging, the coils were sparking in their rhythm, and sounding like a 'whip cracking' convention. Jan edged towards the cage and gingerly entered. Once inside he could feel the ubiquitous energy – somehow, different this time?

He sat for a few minutes, he was feeling something, but it was nowhere near as powerful as before. He sat for a bit longer, and then decided to exit the cage and shutdown the rig. By the end Jan was quite pleased that he had managed to tame the energy within the cage, but - was it too much?

Later he composed an email to Charlie, to describe his findings and to put forward his thoughts on further progression with the experiment. Very soon after he sent it, Charlie replied and said that it would probably be best if came round, so that they could work it out together.

The next afternoon, Charlie and Jan were in the lab discussing what to do next.

'I've got a couple of ideas Jan, but it's probably best to try them out, one at a time.'

Firstly, they started to experiment with repositioning the Graphene sheets within the cage. Charlie had already worked this one out in his head, to what was the best way to place them. As always though, all good ideas need fine tuning. Eventually, using some monitoring tech equipment and common sense, they felt that they had found the best placement for the sheets.

Once again Jan sat in the cage and Charlie fired up the rig. As usual, a low hum emitted from the rig and the coils sparked with super sharp bursts of lightning energy. The energy in the air was heavy, as if they could almost cut through it with a knife. The coils also made the usual cracking sound, but this time the sound was more subdued and almost sounded busy like.

'That's a slightly different sound, maybe we've managed to finally channel all the energy through the cage at last?' Remarked Jan. Indeed - they had set up a two-stage system with the sheets, with equal amounts on the outside of the cage, and on the inside of the cage. Charlie worked out, that this way the energy might be more regulated within the cage. The amount of regulation could also be controlled by changing the sheet ratio inside, and outside the cage.

'Can you feel anything Jan?'

'It's weird, I can hear you okay, but it's almost like I'm sitting in a glass bubble and somehow detached from you and the outside.'

'Well, I think that's good - maybe?' Said Charlie, as he slightly shrugged his shoulders.

'Fancy a cup of tea then Charlie?'

'Yes - great! I'll tell you about my other idea if you have some biscuits as well.'

Jan then went off to make the tea.

On his return, he suddenly remarked:

'It better be a bloody good idea Charlie - because I'm giving you some chocolate hobnobs.'

'It's tailored especially for your mad idea of - going beyond, with this thing.'

Charlie went on to explain that the idea followed the principles of a so-called electronic spirit box...

'This is what paranormal investigators often use for voice contact with "the other side" - apparently,' explained Charlie.

'My idea Jan is to incorporate a similar scanning circuit into the rig that the 'spirit box' uses. If we can somehow make the coils quickly scan in frequency like the spirit box does, then it might get you closer to where you want to be?' Obviously, this idea was going to take some time, probably a few weeks according to Charlie. With this, Jan thought it best to catch up with a few outstanding jobs first - if only to keep the peace indoors.

On a hot afternoon, a few days later, Jan was in the lab with the rig switched on. He was tinkering around with the test rig, cleaning and checking all the connections and all that. Chloe suddenly popped her head in the doorway and shouted:

'I've cut some sandwiches off - if you're hungry?'

'Yeah, sure - I'll be right in.'

After a couple of minutes, Jan headed indoors.

'What have we got then?'

'Cheese and egg, that's it - we aren't the high earners anymore!'

'I really don't mind what they are. Any sandwich with a packet of prawn cocktail crisps - is a GREAT meal to me!' Announced Jan.

'Okay. Can you stand away from the radio, I want to hear the news headlines please Jan.'

Jan moved to the side, and they both listened to the news.

'It's the same old rubbish, we're at the mercy of the media. They make up, and curtail a lot of the content most of the time anyway!'

'Yeah, whatever,' came back Chloe.

'Anyway, did you tune in the station properly Clo? It sounds like there is someone else talking on the radio every now and then.'

'No. I know what you are saying though, it's always tuned to that station, I haven't touched it,' Jan just shrugged his shoulders and headed back to the lab.

On entering the lab, Jan looked around and noticed that he had left the rig on, with the coils gently humming and sparking away. *Might as well try the cage out again, as I forget to turn it off. It's certainly warmed up now!* He started to climb in and forgot himself as he entered. Stupidly, he held onto the outer caging as his foot touched the earthed floor. The next thing he knew, he was coming around from what seemed like a sleep, but he was lying on the floor of the cage! *Oh my god! That was stupid of me - I'll not to do that again!'*

Charlie paid Jan a visit again a couple of days later, to fit the scanning card into the test rig. It did take quite a while though to get it to fire up and to work harmoniously within the original working circuit.

'Wow!' They both shouted when the system got up to speed.

'It sounds like a steam train going at full pelt Jan!'

'It's mad! It's like we are back at the beginning of the industrial revolution - but in a "Back To The Future" kinda way.' They just stood in awe for a few seconds.

'Do you fancy giving it a go then Jan?'

'Err - yes I'll give it a go. I forgot to tell you this but the last time that I tried going into the cage, I was sparked out. I accidently touched the live side of the cage as I entered.'

'Oh My! I hope the panic button worked?'

'Yes, you kinda saved my life in a way Charlie.'

'Well, - thank you. How long were you out for?'

'This is the thing - It seemed like - just a few seconds. According to the clock though - it was about forty minutes.'

'That's weird Jan.'

'Well, that's not all. I've only just remembered this, but while I was out of it, I could faintly see a black path within a dark tunnel. It looked like I was standing on it – although, I was really lying on the floor of the cage. I wanted to walk along the path, but when I tried, I couldn't grip the path. Somehow, none of it seemed like a dream to me!'

'Bloody hell Jan, are sure that the rig was not still on?'

'It was still working when I came round Charlie. I'm sorry that I lied!'

Chapter Five

'I hate to say this Charlie, but there doesn't seem to be any change in here!'

'That's strange, and frankly - a bit of a let-down.'

'Well, I've been in here for around three minutes. I'll give it a couple more, then I'll come out.'

Nothing changed in the next few minutes, so they decided to call it a day. Charlie headed home and both of them agreed that they would be in touch at some point.

'Did you and Charlie try to get something out of that cage set up, today then?'

'Well, today, Chloe, we thought that we had done enough to make it a truly unique experiment. It's definitely doing something in there! The trouble is nobody has a clue what to expect. It might be as far as a human can hopefully expect to go? For some reason I remember that I was warned about this in a dream a while ago.'

'I remember that a little while back you were telling me that you had all the answers and GIVE me back some of the bedcovers.'

'You're right Clo, I seem to have forgotten the very thing that all the technology in the world can't provide. I've kinda got swept away with all the excitement of adding all the extra parts.'

They both then fell into their sleep.

I must learn to relax and concentrate.
I must learn to relax and concentrate.
I must learn to relax and concentrate.

Said Charlie over and over to himself, whilst he was sitting in the cage the next day and trying to make it all work.

A little while later he opened his eyes. *Oh, that's about right, I've only fallen asleep while trying to relax here. I just can't seem to find a way through, the only time that I felt something had happened, is when I got sparked out...*

For the rest of the week Jan didn't try to fire up the cage anymore, he thought that the best thing he could do would be to have a rethink. *Mm, thinking about it, maybe I should devise a way that I can somehow receive a controlled shock whilst I'm in the cage. I'm so curious about what I saw last time I was sparked out. Getting knocked out again might be the only way to quickly fall into a concussive hypnotic state again?*

There was no way that Jan wanted to risk getting another big electric shock, so he had to think of a way to receive a mild shock - without it being a danger to his life! This was a difficult one, as he didn't really think that 'safe' was conceivable as being in the same context as 'electric shock'. Charlie was not consulted either as Jan didn't want him to be party to any form of risk taking of someone else's safety. Eventually Jan came up with a possible solution. This involved a timed pulse of moderate voltage whilst he was inside the cage - so another switch had to be incorporated within the cage.

Developing the 'self-induced' shock switch took some experimenting to get right, this was partly down to 'only' using measuring devices to get the perceived voltage about right for human testing. All this was open to interpretation though, as Jan didn't really know how much power was required to kill himself? He obviously decided to work with a minimal induced power to start with, knowing that he could always slightly increase it as needed…

All this further experimentation involved the rig being switched on for prolonged periods of time. Which meant Jan often left it all running whilst he went in for a cup of tea or a meal. It was on one such occasion that he decided to break for a cuppa, he switched on the kettle, scavenged some biscuits, then went to the loo. On his return he could hear sounds coming from the radio as he re-entered the kitchen. He couldn't make out at first what the sounds were, but he froze when the word came out again - 'Janny' in a woman's voice. *That sounded like - no way - it can't be. Is all this starting to get to me mentally.* Jan walked to the radio to turn it off - It was already turned off! At this point, Chloe came in.

'What ya up to?'

'Nothing much, did you leave the radio on when you left the room Clo?'

'No. I haven't turned it on at all today!'

'I just heard something weird coming from the radio as I came into the kitchen.'

'What was that then?'

'This is crazy - but it sounded like my Mum calling me 'Janny'. Nobody ever called me that - only her, and only when I was very young. I must be cracking up - I guess?'

'It's so easy when you hear something unexpectedly, to bend and interpret it, to a familiar word - a bit like hearing your mobile phone ring when listening to music in the car. You then turn down the car radio - to silence - no call. I guess while you are doing a weird experiment with all that noise in your lab, it might play a similar trick to your ears?'

'Yes, it's kinda what I was thinking also Clo.'

'You're starting to play with fire - in a Hellish way, Jan.'

'Yes, thanks.'

Jan headed off to the lab, with tea and biscuits in hand. *Relaxed mode - check. Panic button - check, fingers trembling over induction switch - check!*

Two minutes later, Jan came around. *Bloody hell - it worked, although I was still aware of my surroundings of the cage and coils and stuff! Perhaps an extra 10% on the power settings will completely kick me in?*

A little while later, he tried again. Almost straight away, he was in, and back - looking at the dark tunnel and black pathway. There was nothing else, not even a pinpoint of a light source! *Oh My God! I can't believe it - I was right - I'm back looking at what I saw before. Can this all be a dream?* There was utter silence, it was almost painful to Jan as he had not experienced anything so quiet before. Like the first time when Jan had seen this place, he was standing, - although - really, he was still seated back in the cage. *Right! This time I'm going to try and walk on the pathway again.* His feet appeared that they were in contact with the path, but try as he might, he wasn't going anywhere! His walking kind of looked like a small animal doing a walking motion, even though it was being held up above the ground. He was so determined to proceed along the pathway that he forgot his concentration and accidentally hit the panic button. Immediately! - He returned. He was OK and had no after effects from the induction and visit. *That's it - I've managed to do it! Am I the first to go and see - whatever it was? He couldn't stop thinking about it. Where is that place? Is it real? Have I fallen into an elaborate hoax or dream? I'm guessing that there's only one way to find out - to keep going with the experiment...*

Although he was giddy with excitement, he decided to give himself a bit of time to think about whether he should tell Chloe and Charlie.

After a little while though, he thought it best to establish some more facts about his journey, so he set about, to actually find out some proof if others had witnessed anything similar to himself.

That evening he conducted an online search about what he had witnessed earlier on that day. After sifting through a lot of the search engine results, he finally came across something that could be of interest?

"There has been described by some, who have witnessed some ancient Egyptian 'Funerary Manuscripts'. Images of a dark tunnel, which according to some, to be a crossing to the afterlife. These books known as the 'Book Of The Dead' were sometimes placed in burial tombs, around two thousand years ago."

That's it! It's real! Or at least it might have been in ancient Egyptian times... However, somebody else knows about it, so somebody must have also witnessed it. Jan just had to let somebody know about what he had seen. He thought that telling Chloe would be too lengthy and complicated. He instead sent a message to Charlie - after all he had already told Charlie about the tunnel before.

It wasn't long before he was back in the lab again and sitting in the cage. *Oh my, it's so quiet in here, the lack of sound pressure almost hurts my ears. Reaching his feet down again, Jan tried to walk - it was still hopeless. I think that I'll give up on that for a while!*

All of a sudden:

'Janny.'

'Mum. Mum. MUM.'

'You don't need to shout or speak in here sweetheart.'

'But Mum - I can't see you. Please tell me that I can?'

'I'm so sorry sweetheart, you won't be able to see us, we've moved on too far.'

'I love you! Please be there for me, when it's time.'

'Me and your Father have always been by your side Janny.'

At this point tears were rolling down Jan's cheeks. He was so shocked and emotional, that he pressed the panic switch. Suddenly, he was back to reality. The utter shock of hearing his mother's voice again shook him into silence - In thought and in audible mutterings. Now feeling utterly exhausted and tired, he headed off to take some rest.

'Come on sleepy, it's nearly teatime.' Spoke Chloe in a soft toned voice as she gently shook him.

'Oh, hi Clo, I was out of it!'

'You're probably spending too much time in that lab of yours by the look of it.'

'Yeah, I'm going to have to break away from it, I guess. It's like I'm slowly getting consumed by it all.'

'What we need is a day out. How about taking a picnic to the beach or something?'

'Okay, how about tomorrow then Clo? It's as good a time as any.'

Off they went to the beach the next day, the sun was shining (behind the clouds anyway) Once at their destination, they choose their spot on the pebble beach. They quickly unfolded the picnic mat - before it blew away in the wind...

'It's a bit fresh sitting here, isn't it Clo?'

'It doesn't matter Jan, we're together and we are having fun.'

'You know, coming out for just even a few hours has made me feel so refreshed! Being at home has started to compress on me a bit. When I'm in the lab, it kinda makes me feel like I've caught a mild case of flu, aching muscles and slight headaches and such-the-like.'

'Perhaps, you might be better off finding something else worthwhile to do. Maybe earn a bit of money Jan, also we need to get out more! Swap the walls for the hedgerows, and all that!'

Jan thought that this was a good time to mention his recent experience of hearing his mother. This was rather going against what he had decided earlier though - not to tell Chloe about it!

'I've already messaged Charlie about it. In his reply, he thought that all the power being produced in the lab was possibly having a brain altering, hallucinogenic effect on my thoughts.'

'I'll go with Charlie on that. You don't know what effect it's having on you. It would probably be safer sticking your head in the microwave, if you ask me.'

Jan nodded in agreement, obviously though, he wasn't going to take a word of it in.

A few days later, Jan was back in the lab. He thought he would take advantage of the fact that it was Chloe's day at work - to minimise any possible questioning later.

'Mum, are you there?' There was just silence.

'Mum, can you hear me - please,' - nothing!

'Please, can you hear me?'

'Voices are not usually heard here Janny. I have your father by my side.'

Oh my God - Dad! Jan decided at this point to answer in thought only.

'Yes, son. We love you and will always love you!'

But! - How can you hear me?

'Like your mother said Jan, this is no place for the physical, we are beyond the realms of physicality.'

Jan had now understood what his parents were saying. Wherever he and they were, did not abide by the physical requirements to move and communicate. *I just have to think about my questions and conversations to communicate in this place.* Unfortunately, by the time Jan had figured it out, he was back into the reality of physical world again. Again, like before, the whole short experience had drained Jan, so he had to sit down and take some rest.

By the time Jan had regained some energy it was getting towards evening time and the lab had developed a slight chill. *Aw, I've been waiting for this, it's finally cold enough for an excuse to light my lab woodburner!* Having already spent weeks - in anticipation of this moment, he had already organised the sequence of fire lighting. Surprisingly, the woodburner was soon heating up and starting to take the chill from the air. Jan just sat there looking at the machine, thinking about what to do next. Does he periodically turn it on so that he can nip in to visit his Mum and Dad? *That is just so weird that I don't even know where to begin with that one! He thought to himself. This is all uncharted territory, I shouldn't even be doing this, is it even ethical? He was still making his mind up if the whole thing was a big hallucination. Have I just spent a load of money and time on a big 'tripping' machine? Whatever it is, I certainly never expected to speak to my parents again - ever!*

The next thing he knew was that the Sun was shining in his eyes and a Blackbird was in full song outside the Lab, it was almost making his ears bleed. *Bloody Hell. What is the time?* Looking at his phone it read: 04.45.

Jumping up, he thought that he had a good chance to get into bed before Chloe woke up.

Removing his clothes prior to entering the bedroom, and being as quiet as possible whilst entering the bed, Chloe opened her eyes:

'Morning, did you get lost on the way to bed last night?'

'Well actually, I lit the woodburner last night, and the next thing I knew, I was waking up about five minutes ago.'

'How about inviting me over, next time you get all cosy in there?'

'Yeah, sorry Clo, we should have lit the first fire together I guess.'

'Next time?'

They both then went back to sleep for a couple of hours. Jan decided to give the lab a rest for a while, until Chloe was next at work - at least.

Around a week later he decided that he couldn't wait any longer. As soon as Chloe left for work, he headed straight to the lab and switched it all on. At this point, Jan kinda knew what to expect from switching on the rig. This was - very little, until the coils had heated up to allow more free resonance - or something like that?

This gave him the opportunity to nip back inside the house and make some tea and breakfast for himself. Jan considered himself old school - meaning that he couldn't really function first thing in the morning unless he'd had a cup of tea. The tea had to be sweetened with at least three sugars, or he wouldn't be able to fire on all cylinders. Grabbing his tea and toast, he was about to exit the kitchen when all of a sudden, a very distorted 'Love You' came from the kitchen radio.

Jan quickly ran from the kitchen to the lab - dropping his toast and spilling most of his tea on the way. He jumped on the chair in the cage - hitting the shock button and he was in.

Mum, Dad…

…Mum, Dad. Was it you that said 'love you' through the kitchen radio?

…Please can you hear me…

After some time of calling for his parents within his thoughts, Jan couldn't help it, but he just had to shout:

'PLEASE, MUM, DAD, SPEAK TO ME!'

Chapter Six

After calling for his parents for what seemed hours, Jan decided to eventually give up. Suddenly another voice came through:

'They've had to finally let go Jan.'

'WHAT! - Who is this?'

'I've been in the background and I'm very impressed with what you have accomplished so far Jan.'

'IVOR.'

'Please don't use your voice Jan, it's dangerous!'

Thinking carefully about what he was doing, Jan went back into inner thought communication.

I can't believe this! Where are we Ivor? Why can't I see you or anyone else? Although Jan had accomplished his goal - so far, of reaching the - other side, there wasn't anything to be seen – as yet?

'It's all in your mind Jan. Just like everything has always been!'

I don't understand, what does that mean Ivor? Is this reality, or am I dreaming?

'It's less defined here, than it is in - what we call life. All I can say is that you are breaking a rule, and it will not be tolerated under any circumstance!'

Tolerated - by whom?

'I'm new here Jan and I'm hardly able to understand, let alone explain.'

You said that my parents had to - 'finally let go'.

'At this time, my understanding of it all, is that your parents - who have passed for several years now, have probably almost gone through the whole process and are now nearly ready to move on again. I'm guessing it was a real struggle for them to make contact with you?'

How did they know that I was here?

'It's called love, Jan. It remains with you; the love of Mother and child is the strongest bond of all. Now that you have made contact with them, they now probably feel that they are ready to move on. I'm guessing that it was a lovely thing for them.'

Where have they moved onto Ivor?

'I don't know Jan. From what I understand about it, many of your memories remain when you pass. However, most of these will fade quickly though, as you travel through. The speed that you travel through is dependent on how quickly you can clear your memories. Most do not want to hang around here, which appears to be an intermediary stage. Some cleanse their memories quickly, most though, find it hard to clear the memory of a loved one. You can choose one thing though, and that is to wait until your nearest and dearest pass or make contact. This is an unusual concession. I'm guessing that now your parents have made final contact, they are fulfilled and want to move on. I'm told that when the living makes positive contact with their deceased relatives - say through a medium, those that have passed, soon move on after, so I'm just putting two and two together Jan.' Jan fell silent for a few seconds and then replied:

I'm sorry Ivor, I can't take this all in. I have to go now!

Jan was back in his lab again. This time he wasn't so upset as he was when he first contacted his parents. This time he was in utter disbelief, shocked and staring in a fixed eye-trance like state. He headed indoors and made straight for the bedroom. He climbed on the bed and laid down in a semi dazed state. He had a lot to think about. *This is all getting rather heavy now. Have I gone too far? Will I be punished when it's my turn to pass on?* Eventually after asking himself about another dozen questions, he calmed down slightly and started to nap.

After what seemed a very short time in his sleep, the slamming of a car door woke him up. *Chloe, she's back, it must be past five o'clock.* Sure enough, it was, so Jan quickly jumped into the shower. This act of quickly taking a shower seemed the best solution for Jan - for a bit of classic pretence.

'Knock, knock! It's only me.'

'Hi Clo, I didn't hear you pull up.'

'I guess that you wouldn't hear me whilst you are taking a shower - silly boy! I've only just noticed - but, have you lost a bit of weight? Are you feeling alright, or worrying about anything?'

'No, no,' he replied while looking at his tummy at the same time. 'I guess that I've been eating less - which is good, while I've been so busy.'

Jan hadn't really noticed, but after looking at himself in the mirror, it did appear - even to himself, that he had lost some weight.

Time was up for Jan - for the next day anyway, until Chloe went to work again. This was just as well because he was exhausted, together with a splitting headache. While he was in this state there was only one thing for it, and that was to get an early night. He didn't even bother about any dinner.

The next day Jan was feeling a little bit more refreshed, so he set about catching up on all of the jobs that needed doing, he even found some time to go out with Chloe.

Come the following day, a pattern was starting to emerge for him. To add to this emerging pattern of events Jan pretended to be dozing whilst Chloe got ready for work, in the morning time. He only 'fully' woke up when she was about to leave. Kissing her goodbye and waiting until she had left in the car, he then got dressed and headed straight for the lab. Once inside he started the process of warming up the cage. *Breakfast time! Fry up today, as I want to find out some answers.* In the kitchen Jan set about a 'full works' fry up. He switched on the radio - half expecting something to come through straight away. Nothing did! A little while later the mega breakfast was ready; four slices of toast, jam, pot of tea, three sausages, four rashes of bacon, three fried eggs, two large fried tomatoes, three hash browns and baked beans. He tucked in, and by the end, he had nearly licked the plate clean - surprisingly! Feeling quite disappointed that no message had come through on the radio speaker, he got up and puffed quite a lot, turned off the radio and headed to the lab.

Ivor, are you there? It would be great to hear you and speak to you again.

There was no reply. Jan carried on calling Ivor every few minutes for about the next half an hour. Thinking about giving up, he heard a 'HA' in the distance.

It was you at your wake wasn't it Ivor?

'Yes, I was there.'

How can you even start to get your head around being present at your own funeral?

'Oh, it seems kinda normal, everyone who passes, visits their own funeral.'

Weren't you overcome with grief?

'That would have been a question that I would have certainly asked. How can I say it – yes, it's a bit like dreading to do something, but it turns out that you actually like it once you try it! Well, passing is like that, the thrill and rush you get together with an overpowering sense of calm, warmth and love is off the scale! It's all encompassing! Now I'm here and looking back - at what I can remember, is like wanting to go back to a plague ridden, dark, cold and starved time. You just don't want to go back!'

Don't you miss Ellen and your kids?

'Not here - now, I'm starting to lose the emotion of love, maybe it's because I know It's not the end - so it's all good! Even those of the living who believe in moving on, still have a fear of dying. It's a natural emotion - for the living. However, I now know that there is nothing to fear, and I see it as a relief when you pass - a lifting of many burdens for most. But! I still believe in a full physical life for all.'

Why the hell aren't the living told that there is nothing to fear?

'The whole merry-go-round of evolution would grind to a halt if one dimension, world - or whatever, had insight to the next or previous one. Above all of this, is the survival instinct and urge to move on. My time here hasn't taught me anything more about God or such-the-like. I have, however, got some way to go. I don't know what to expect?'

Well, I still can't believe that I'm actually talking to you Ivor? Wouldn't you like to make contact with Ellen and your children?

'I have no more of an idea than you Jan, if you 'are' actually talking to me. All anyone can do, and believe in, is their pathway to carry on in the universe. It's like a virtual conveyor belt, I guess. It would be lovely to hear from Ellen and the kids, but I'm happy to get through here as quickly as possible. I'm settled in my mind, now that I know the fate of most physical lives. There is one caveat though - which I'm sure was never meant to be, is that at the moment of a sudden and tragic death, some are able to - hop off the conveyor. I saw it myself - like in the corner of my vision, a small circular light source. Apparently, as soon as you choose to head forward to the main light and start to move forward, the small circular exit - if you like, disappears.'

So, it's true then, about light at the end of the tunnel?

'That's kinda what I experienced; it could be that it's different for everybody though. I've been told, that if you do decide to 'hop off' that it's 'true' suicide for your eternal soul. Yes, you will still be able to roam the earth in spirit form, but when all of your energy has depleted it's "Goodnight Vienna" - apparently.'

How long can your energy last then?

'Well, maybe the younger you are, the longer you last? No more than a few hundred years - maybe.'

Do you know how many 'hop off', then Ivor?

'My estimate is around half of all the newly deceased Jan.'

So, where are we now then Ivor?

'That is a tricky one Jan! You – yourself, are witnessing the tunnel.'

What! The very tunnel about which we were just talking about.

'Yes, it's much more than a tunnel though. Every soul is moving forward here - as I mentioned before. However, we can all be anywhere at any time within the tunnel though. We all have a default location within the tunnel as well, until we move on. Put it this way -

when you have a body to haul about, you can only move slowly and obviously only be in one place at once. Have you ever in your dreams been somewhere, then a blink later you're somewhere totally different?'

Yes of course, many times Ivor!

'Well, it's very similar for me here. I don't need to plan about where I want to go, I just think about it and I'm there. This is all done at a much higher frequency than it is when in-body, you move instantly. I'm guessing here, that's because - you are still bound to your physical body - which can't be attenuated to move at a higher frequency, I'm somehow forced to slow down to your level. That's, if I wish to remain in contact with you.'

So, would it be impossible for the living to experience what it's truly like here?

'I can almost guarantee that millions have and - will, get to see what it's really like here at some point.'

I've tried to walk in here before Ivor, I wasn't going anywhere! It was like trying to walk in thin-air.

'As you know, I'm almost as confused as you are about this place Jan. I wouldn't be overly upset about it; you are probably the first physical body to witness this place?'

I've got so many questions, what was it like to die?

'For me, it was seamless, as I had no pain, and I was already asleep anyway. Somehow though, I knew that I had died. I was not panicked by this realisation; it was all calm. I guess though that if I had been killed instantly by the impact with the car, the suddenness of it might have made it all a bit different. I might have wanted to hop off then?'

Does time exist here?

'Apart from thinking and communicating in a given language, nothing from the physical world exists here. All of the physical world's inventions and discoveries are unknown and useless here.'

Ivor you keep saying about 'all in here'. The only people I have heard, are you, and my Mum and Dad. I have yet to see anyone. Do you mix with other souls?

'We only mix when we have to. Instinct drives us Jan, we all kind-of-know what we have to do. We all travel at different levels but can call upon anyone we want. You probably wouldn't believe it though, but there is authority here as well.'

Tell me more?

'Since I've been here, I've been summoned to two personal ecclesia's - the word means something like: meeting. I was told on both occasions that I was not to communicate with the living, if I were to be contacted, I would remain silent. Apparently with the recent advent of technology by the living to break down the barriers, has meant an authoritative measure had to be taken. There are what's called the "gatekeepers", they were the ones that I had to meet. You could call them - the secret police.'

Is that the reason you said earlier, that by using my voice, it could be dangerous?

'Yes, exactly Jan. The gatekeepers are ubiquitous - you never know where they are, even when they are by your side, you don't —

All of a sudden, Jan was back to reality!

'What on earth is going on? Have I just awoken from a bad dream,' Jan mumbled to himself as he tried to get up and out the cage, he wasn't going anywhere though! It was as if most of his body had been paralysed. He could hardly move his arms and upper body; he couldn't even feel his legs! By his own reckoning, he had been trying to contact and 'actually' talking to Ivor for a total of around an hour. Looking at his phone it was nearly midnight - half a day had passed! There was nothing else for it though, Jan had to wait until all his feelings and senses came back. When this would be - he didn't know. He sat there tired and feeling sick, dreading the thought of explaining - again, to Chloe.

Eventually, he was able to become mobile again, this time though, he didn't even bother to go indoors, instead he lit the woodburner and made himself comfortable. He was too tired and weak, to face another showdown with Chloe. *I'm quite cosy here. Maybe I should provide myself with a few more home comforts, perhaps a bed and some washing facilities.*

Luckily for Jan, Chloe was due to go to work again early the next morning. *Hopefully, she might have calmed down by the time she came home from work later in the day,* he thought.

All of a sudden, his phone pinged a text. It read:

You have been warned before in your dreams. IGNORE - BE TAKEN!

Jan looked at the sender's number, it was his own. As Jan's job was in telecommunications, he knew that it was quite possible to send yourself a text. The problem was - he didn't send it himself - as far as he was aware? Someone or something did though, this somewhat started to freak him out. There was no denying that the text was very real! He sat a while and tried to work his way through it, obviously he couldn't, and he felt very discombobulated.

Morning quickly came round. 'Knock, knock,' Jan answered the door:

'Tea. You look a bloody mess! – How about returning the favour by having our evening meal ready for us on the table, when I get home.' Chloe then slammed the door shut again - in fact so hard that it almost smashed the door jamb out of its frame. He thought to himself that it would probably be best to wait until Chloe had gone to work before he even ventured out of his lab. When he did so, it was only to freshen up, he was not hungry and had barely had a slurp of his tea.

Despite being disturbed by the text; Jan was hardly put off. He was aware though, that he was becoming increasingly more consumed and obsessed by it all now. If you could observe him, you would see similarities between him and the obsessed main character - Roy Neary, in the film Close Encounters of the Third Kind.

After he had done what he needed to do in the house, he headed straight back to the lab. Nothing was going to stop him now!

Chapter Seven

Once back in the cage, Jan quickly went through the process to get himself back into the tunnel.

Ivor, I'm back. I don't know what happened back there but one second you were talking, and the next, I was back in the cage?

The next thing that he knew - he was hurtling along the tunnel towards a bright light. Think of the worst roller coaster ride that you have ever been on, and times it by one hundred, that's how the ride was for Jan. Very quickly, he came to a standstill again.

MY GOD. I can see you Ivor! I know it's you, but it doesn't look much like the 'you' that I used to know!

'I had no idea myself that this was going to happen. You appeared and I grabbed your arm and I thought to myself that we must get somewhere safe. You see without a physical body, the soul, spirit, ghost or whatever you want to call it, can take on many visual forms. However, spirits still have individual facial features - like their human face, once seen they can easily be recognised again.'

Jan was looking at a more human representation of Ivor, although it was a bit like it was being projected on a screen by a dodgy old projector.

'YOU WERE WARNED JAN!'

What? - How do you know that Ivor?

The area where they were standing was brightly lit, but it wasn't overpowering. Jan couldn't believe how clear everything was, *this is like being able to see in super high-definition*, he thought to himself. The area appeared to be vast, and it was a total contrast to the dark and deathly silence of the tunnel. No walls or boundaries could be seen, so Jan guessed it could be the size of a small warehouse or as big as the universe? We are talking - other worldly here! All around were lots and lots of dark tunnel entrances. They all seemed to be approximately two-to-three metres in diameter, Jan guessed that these were all probably part of the tunnel network.

A strange low-pitched thrum reverberated everywhere, it seemed to be omni-directional in nature, and the intensity of the sound stayed exactly the same wherever you were. Jan had realised now, that to move around he needed to be in contact with Ivor, otherwise, he would be walking in 'thin air' - again!

'You quickly returned to reality because I sent you back, as I sensed that a gatekeeper was approaching. I didn't see one, but I could see a message was sent to your phone from here. They are getting too-close for comfort! I cut you off, for your own protection.'

That message really shook me up! The more I visit here though, the less - it seems that I want to go back! It's totally weird here Ivor - but so intriguing. Why is it, that the closer that I get to a hole, or tunnel or whatever, the pitch of the thrum seems to change - slightly?

'Each individual has their own pitch or frequency - if you like, which they must follow to lead them down their designated path to the end.'

Yes, it's all very organised Ivor. Tell me - why are we in this particular area?

'There's less chance that a gatekeeper will come in here, they prefer the tunnels. The tunnels offer more privacy and surprise when they interrogate a newly passed.'

Whilst Ivor was explaining this, Jan couldn't help but notice hundreds of balls of lights darting in-and-out of the tunnels. Once the balls of light were inside the tunnels though, no light source could be seen.

'If you get caught - and you will! We are both for it. The best thing is for you to go back! The gatekeepers can't very easily visit the physical world - you would be much safer back there!'

Of course, you are right Ivor! However, I'm starting to get used to it - a bit, here. I want to find out more. When I'm here, I'm totally relaxed and don't seem to have any worries and nagging memories of the physical world, it all seems to be buried deep in my mind. It's like being a carefree child all over again. My body isn't burdened with the constant need to be fed or watered. What's not to like?

'Believe me when I say - you'll be in here quick enough anyway.'

What's the problem then?

'It's not your time yet to leave the physical world.'
Jan pretended to ignore what Ivor had just said.

What I've been wondering is: do you know where we are in relation to my lab?

'That's a matter of opinion Jan. To the best of my knowledge, all I can say is: only the physical world live on the surface of the Earth. Most other worlds and dimensions exist mainly beneath the Earth's surface.

This might be different for you personally though. Who knows where YOU are?'

Beneath the surface; that's bonkers - surely?

'The weather on the surface has a much more important role than to just keep the physical alive. For instance: electrical storms including man made electricity, it all feeds down into the earth eventually. The same is true for water, it also finds its way down into the earth. They are both very important energy sources for all of us, and possibly - others?'

Suddenly: everything just stopped, and everything just stood still.

'YOU WERE WARNED ABOUT RETURNING.' Came a voice out of the ether. It was indiscernible whether it was male or female.

'Who is this?' Said Jan, who couldn't help but shout.

'Janus Alby. I have come to collect you, for your return back to the physical world. You have broken a rule that was created when the Earth was granted life and consciousness for the inhabitants.'

There stood in front of Jan, a human looking figure around five feet tall, long black hair, with a young pure skinned face. However, it was for Jan to decide whether this was a man or woman, the lack of solidity to the body form, made it even harder to tell. One thing was pretty clear to Jan though, that this figure wasn't from the modern world.

Is it you who sent me that text?

'A warning was sent to you. The physical world receives these messages by the most appropriate method.'

How come I can see you? All others are just balls of light.

'You can only see me because - I want you to! Your visual perception of myself is just an image in your mind. No more questions, you have to leave now!'

I thought that I would be 'Taken' if I returned to this place?

'To die is not possible in this world, you have to die in your own world. You will be taken upon your return to the physical world. All of the rest of your life will be lost!'

With these words Jan then hit the panic button. Briefly on his return he saw the insides of his lab. Then nothing!

Sometime later he came-around, he didn't have a clue whether he was alive or dead, if he was dreaming or where he 'really' was! All he did know, was that he was lying down in his own bed. Whether he was 'actually' in his own bed - in his own room, was maybe something that he and 'only' he, could eventually decide. *It's getting to the point now, where my own mind is getting very confused! How on earth do I decide what is real or not?* Jan decided that the best thing to do was to just shut his eyes and relax into a sleep again. Hopefully, this would help to prevent the early onset of madness.

A few hours later he opened his eyes again, this time Chloe was standing by the bedside. Jan immediately looked up and thought to himself: *I never did get round to changing that 'stupid' 1970's curtain pelmet up there!*

'What the hell has happened to you?'

'There's nothing wrong with me,' came Jan's reply.

'Nothing wrong - huh! Why did I find you sparked out on the floor in that stupid cage then? I had to run and fetch John from next door to help me haul you indoors.'

'I guess that I just got a bit over-tired. Is it because I haven't put your dinner on yet?'

'DINNER ON YET! - That was yesterday.'

'Well, what's the problem then?'

'I'll tell you what the problem is: you're spending far too much time sitting in that cage. God knows what you are doing? I haven't seen you eat or drink anything for days - No! I haven't seen YOU for days! You're dirty, gaunt, unshaved and you're becoming withdrawn.'

'Is there anything else that you can think of?'

'Do you have any means of telling the time down there as you don't seem to know whether it's time for bed or not. You've become obsessed with whatever you are doing in that cage, and it's taken control of you - like a drug addict! I've booked you a doctor's appointment for tomorrow, we'll see what he has to say!'

'Just leave me alone.'

Chloe quickly made an exit, slamming the door behind her.

What on earth has rattled her cage? I'm really more concerned about my safety, did I manage to evade the gatekeeper, can they really end it for me now I'm back here?

Jan stayed in the bedroom the rest of the day, looking at the tv and the wallpaper. Staring at the wallpaper acted as a fixed-point focus to do some serious thinking he found. Losing himself in thought, he methodically went through all of the recent events, trying to actually make out whether any of it was serious or not. Is his life in danger? He could almost dismiss all of it, apart from when Ivor had told him about events after his death. To hear someone who is actually dead, tell you about what happened at their own funeral - takes some working around to dismiss. The dominant thought in Jan's head was that he - himself, knew what had happened, so perhaps it was all a dream anyway - as all the facts already existed within his head.

Jan knew that he was going back at the first opportunity anyway, so he thought it best to devise a test. This was going to be difficult because Ivor had to tell Jan something that Jan didn't yet know. The only thing that Jan could think of quickly was to use the doctor's visit as a test for Ivor. His plan was to ask for a blood test, which would take a few days for the results to come through.

The next day Chloe drove Jan to the surgery. For both of them, the five-minute drive never seemed so long, neither of them spoke to each-other on the way - all a bit awkward - they both thought to themselves.

Jan took a seat in the waiting room; he was soon called in to see the doctor.

'Hello Janus, how can I help you?'

'Hello doctor. My wife is concerned that I seem to be a bit stressed. I do seem to be getting tired a lot, and I have lost a bit of weight recently.' The doctor then went through the usual procedure with weighing him and listening to Jan's chest and heart, as well as carrying out a few more routine tests. The doctor then asked Jan quite a few questions - as they do!

'I can't say that there is anything obviously amiss with you Janus. Yes, you've lost some weight and your heart rate is slightly raised. My suggestion is that you take some rest and try to eat a balanced diet.'

Usual advice then! - Jan thought to himself.

'Can I make a request please, doctor?'

'Yes, go ahead Janus.'

'Would it be possible to have a blood test, just to make sure.'

'Well, I can't see what harm it will do. I see it's been a few years since you last had one, it will be a routine blood test - all the normal stuff. Call the surgery for the results in around a week's time.'

'Thank you doctor.'

So, the doctor duly took a sample from Jan's arm.

Having set up the test, Jan knew the difficult part still lay ahead - to get back into the cage within the next few days!

The ice thawed a bit between Chloe and Jan over the next day, helped no doubt by Jan being extra nice and passive to Chloe's requests. He even managed to have a shave, but his first and foremost thing to do was accomplish: 'Operation Cage Revisit' asap! Jan did have as many days as he wanted to really, though, as he realised that until he 'actually' contacted the surgery he might never know the results? At least, until a dreaded thought cloud hovered over him: *I suppose if the results are Bad, they might contact me as soon as possible.*

From that day on, Jan and Chloe seemed to be getting along just fine. Jan was starting to get a bit anxious though and was slightly bubbling under the surface, wondering if he would get to the cage soon or not.

'What shall we have for dinner tonight then Jan.'

'I don't know, and I don't care - I mean - I'm not that hungry Clo.'

'I still haven't seen you eat much since your visit to the doctors.'

'I'm working on it, the appetite still has to come back, fully - I guess.'

'The sooner the better! - I want to see a bit more meat on them-their bones!'

There came a knock at the door. Chloe answered, it was Ellen. Chloe invited her in to join them for a cup of tea. They all sat down. Jan wasn't overly talkative though. Eventually the conversation crept round to him.

'How have you been Jan, I haven't seen much of you lately?' Enquired Ellen.

'Yeah, I've been keeping myself busy in the lab - you know.'

'Are you still experimenting with all the coil things and electricity?'

'Yeah, I'm tinkering around, just trying to re-purpose them.'

'Ivor did tell me a bit about what you are trying to do in that 'lab' of yours.'

'How much did he tell you Ellen?'

'Oh, he said something ridiculous like - "Jan's going to try and contact the dead" or something like that. I said to Ivor "Good luck to Jan with that, once you're gone - you're gone", I told him. I personally don't believe in any ghosts, spirits or the afterlife!'

'Wise words, from a wise woman. I think that men in particular have a fascination with the unknown, it can be seen as an instinctive primeval challenge - I guess. That also includes me, but after doing some research, I'm fairly sure that the only true reality is - the here and now!'

With this, Chloe chipped in:

'But you seem so convinced that you have seen evidence of another world in your lab Jan?'

'Yes, I thought I did, but I'm fairly convinced that it's all that energy being induced into the air that's somehow causing my brain to hallucinate - somehow.'
Ellen quickly interjected:

'So, what did you see then Jan, real or not?'

'Well, the image that I hallucinated was just a dark tunnel, which was totally silent. That's it!'

'If that, was it, I would have considered all that effort and money to have been wasted - if it was me,' Ellen replied. Chloe jumped onto the end of Ellen's words with:

'So does that mean that you're done messing about in that lab of yours?'

'Well, I can't see the point of taking it any further, my dear. I have plans to sell the whole setup, but I still need to carry out some tests to ensure that it's all running as safely as possible.'

'I say the sooner the better that you wrap the whole ridiculous idea up,' replied Chloe.

A little while later, Ellen left. Jan just sat there thinking that Ellen's visit had worked in his favour. He kind of surprised himself by throwing them both off the track in the ad-lib way that he did. This was soon put straight by Chloe when she re-entered the room after seeing Ellen out.

'Something tells me that you're not fully telling the truth about how things really are Jan?'

'To be honest with you Clo, I'm not sure about anything at this particular time. I still don't know what is real or not, so I have to be pragmatic about all this, and put it all down to a scientific reason for what I have seen.'

'Well, that makes sense - I suppose?'

'I mean what I said though, that I'm going to sell it.'

'I don't really want you going in that thing again.'

'It's possible to run it at a much lower power level, which would then be very much safer for me to run!'

'If that's really possible, I'd be much happier for you to wrap it all up then. I'm trusting you with what you have just told me!'

'It's no big deal Clo, I just need a few days to sort it all out.'

'I think that there should be someone in there with you at all times - for your own safety.'

'If you happen to go out when I'm running it, I'll ask Charlie to pop by.'

'I don't know about that, I've got a busy week next week, so you better get on the phone to him soon!'

'Yep, I'm going to start getting organised tomorrow Clo. I thought that you had to go to work at some point this week?'

'No, things have changed around, like I said, I have a busy week, next week. I've been nominated for some training; however, the event location is still to be confirmed. It's possible that I might have to stay in a hotel for a couple of nights.'

'Okay Clo, hopefully, you can find out quickly.' Jan said this while thinking to himself: *That's kinda put pay*

to me making a quick visit to Ivor then! Hopefully,
Chloe 'will' have to stay away next week then.

Chapter Eight

Jan decided to still keep a low 'lab' profile over that weekend, as he was sure that he would have ample time the following week to visit Ivor. Unfortunately for him, Chloe received a text on Sunday night to inform her that her training event had been cancelled at the last minute.

'Oh, What! They've cancelled the training event and I have to go in as normal tomorrow.'

'That's a bit short notice Clo.' *How on earth do I manage to get enough time in the cage now then? I'll have to try wearing my watch, so that I can set the alarm - if it will work in Ivor's world that is?*

'But,'- shouted Chloe. 'The training is taking place later on in the week, apparently I'll be able to commute.'

'Sounds like the Library service is trying to save money?' Shouted Jan in response.

Monday morning came, and as soon as Chloe left for work Jan carried out his usual routine with warming up the cage, but this time he didn't prepare any breakfast - as his appetite had yet to return. Setting the alarm on his watch for four o'clock in the afternoon he jumped into the chair in the cage, and sparked himself in.

Ivor, are you here? There was no reply for quite a while.

'I'm here Jan. You are taking a big risk coming back!'

I thought that the gatekeeper may have captured you?

'I could see the gatekeeper coming towards us, I had to disappear - VERY fast! I had no time to alert you - which I'm sorry for. As I've said before, things happen much quicker here! I'm now keeping a low profile by not sticking to my path, and I'm also trying to stay in the recharging chambers. I was very surprised when I saw the gatekeeper approaching us in a chamber. What surprised me even more is the fact that 'you' were confronted by the gatekeeper - in a chamber!'

All of a sudden, like the roller-coaster ride before, Jan found himself yet again hurtling along the tunnel towards a light area. Once again Jan found himself in this perpetual ultra-clear chamber of tunnel endings and beginnings. 'Mega Cathedral' would be a more appropriate description for what he could again see, he thought to himself.

'This is the middle section of a chamber; we should be safe here,' came Ivor's voice as Jan slowed down to a stop. Jan could now see Ivor again, just the same as before, although, slightly different - maybe slightly younger looking and slightly less defined as Ivor - somehow?

Are we in the middle of the 'Charging Chamber' that you mentioned just now?

'Yes, do you remember how I told you about how all lives need energy.'

Well, yes Ivor.

'It's where we all have to pass through - not only to switch to our specific tunnel but to recharge ourselves as well. After all, we are just balls of energy - I think?'

So, all of the electricity returning to the earth, kinda gets processed in these chambers?

'Yes, that's the way I see it, anyway.'

At this point, Jan remembered that he had been wearing a watch. He gazed down at it, and indeed it was still working - only - much faster! Observing it for a minute or two, Jan came to the conclusion – after counting in his head, that one minute here was equivalent to around ten minutes in the real world. If this was right, he only had around fifty minutes in total to visit Ivor's world. *I hope that this watch remains true to 'reality time' I'll have to play safe and leave after around thirty minutes.*

'My guess is as good as yours Jan.'

What do you mean?

'What you were thinking to yourself just then, about the two different times.'

Do you think that this world inspired the underground system - somehow?

'Well, I know what you are saying Jan. I suppose that there's a possibility, we'll never know I guess.'

I came back here to ask you an important question, Ivor.

'Oh, what's that then?'

Well firstly, I need to know if this is real or not. When I was at home last week, I devised a test.

'Tell me, what was that then Jan?'

The whole idea is for you to tell me, Ivor!

'I haven't a clue!'

Weren't you with me - following me the whole time!

'No. Who do you think you are?'

Well, that was a waste of time. Didn't you see where I went?

'No, but I can take-a-look, if you want Jan?'

What do you mean 'You can take-a-look back?'

'Doctor's visit, was it?'

Jan was absolutely flabbergasted at Ivor's reply.

I'm lost for words. H-how can you possibly have looked back at that?

'Well Jan, some people believe in destiny - which is true. What the living don't realise is that their destiny path doesn't disappear once they have travelled down it. Do you remember when I told you about following your pitch here?'

Yes, of course!

'When you come here Jan, you can sometimes revisit anyone's past - if you know what frequency they are on - of course! My theory is that the path you follow here is just a continuation of your destiny.'

So, what you are saying is, that our lives are laid out before us in the physical world, and in here?

'I've only got the same knowledge as you Jan, plus what I've seen - so far - here. As you know though, memories and knowledge are fading all the time here.'

It's kinda like everyone is at the mercy of dementia in both world's - Great! This is truly mental.

'You also gave a sample of blood, for testing.'

Yes, can you tell me anything about what they may have found out?

'All I can see is something about the red blood cells - possibly?'

Can you give me more detail Ivor?

'Sorry.'

How come when there's anything to find out about another world, there's always very little detail.

Anyway, you passed my test Ivor. This now means that I'll definitely have to call the surgery now!

'I wouldn't worry about it Jan, I probably got the wrong test.'

Is that meant to be some kinda joke Ivor?

'Ivor? - Who? Oh yes.'

Didn't you just say that you could follow anyone's path, if you know what frequency they are on?

'Yes, I think so.'

Meaning that it's unlikely you got my test mixed up with anybody else's then?

'Yes, you must be right Jan, although I've already forgotten what we were talking about?'

I've just thought of something! Could you visit me at any time in the physical world - even in my bedroom?

'In theory – yes, but it would take a huge amount of energy, which would be very draining. It would be much easier if I was invited back, especially by a loved one in a place I have travelled before.'

So, would it be easier to go back to a place that your destiny timeline has crossed?

'Yes. I think that you are right Jan.'

Tell me Ivor, why are you risking yourself for me? Are you also deliberately holding yourself back from moving along your path?

'Yes, I am preventing myself from moving on along my path. To be honest Jan, I enjoy being able to meet up with you here. The thing is though, I still have a lot of my memory left of the physical world. I'm still aware that you are my friend and all of the loved ones that I've left behind - they're fine! What you have done is a first - as far as I know? Look, I'm happy to be part of what you are doing, it's exciting and dangerous at the same time, it's like we're kinda living in a big movie - well - one of us is, although, it's going to hurt sooner or later. I think that it's best for you to quit while you're ahead - before it's too late!'

I feel the same way as you do Ivor, the more I visit here, the longer I want to stay. It's intriguing and truly a physical world first! I feel like some kind of astronaut - boldly going where no-one has gone before.

'It's all very exciting to you because you know that you can leave at any time. I can't leave and I don't really have any feelings about if I like it here or not, this place does not allow you that pleasure. All I know is that I'm moving on to, hopefully, something more wholesome - maybe a Heaven?'

I totally understand Ivor. When I was confronted by the gatekeeper, they said to me that my life would be taken, but not here though, as it wasn't possible.

'I would say that they were right. How can you die in a place where nothing physically lives?'

As soon as Ivor had finished talking, Jan's watch alarm sounded.

I'd better be off Ivor.

'Well, have a good life Jan. Please don't say that you're returning.'

Yes, I'm planning to, hopefully, tomorrow - if my watch is still working properly!

'This can't keep going on Jan. I would like to show you something though.'

Jan pressed the panic button, he disappeared instantly.

Back in his lab, Jan looked at his watch, it was two o'clock in the afternoon. *That went well!* Jan thought to himself. Things weren't that well though, he couldn't move - the physical world was quickly catching up in him. *Oh, my goodness, I haven't felt this bad since I downed a couple bottles of red wine, a while back! Please! Let this all wear off before Clo returns.* Then he remembered what Ivor had said to him about the blood test results. *Oh, please let this all be a dream! I'll give up this stupid experiment - just make everything normal - please!*

As he had limited his time for his visit to Ivor, things seemed to start to wear off quite quickly. After a little while, he became a bit more mobile, and he headed back indoors. Instantly he noticed a flashing 'message' light on his telephone. He pressed the playback button:

'Hello Mr Alby, it's the surgery here, we have received the results of your recent blood test. Could you please give us a call to book an appointment with the doctor?' This didn't sound great to Jan; with a thumping heartbeat he then called the surgery and arranged an appointment for the next day.

On the following day, Tuesday, Jan attended his appointment at the surgery. The doctor asked Jan a few questions, then he informed Jan that he indeed 'did' have an abnormal red blood cell count. It didn't really come as any surprise to Jan, though. The doctor then booked him in for a course of injections to start off with. He was then told not to worry, and sent on his way.

What was peculiar, was that Jan wasn't too worried about it - anyway, as he already knew that there was a problem - of course! What did bother him more though, was he was due to meet up with Ivor again, however, this was now off the cards as it was mid-afternoon, which meant it was too late!

Once Jan was home from the doctors, he settled down on the sofa with a cup of tea and some biscuits. As Jan was almost normal in some-ways, he decided to check his emails again - as it was at least a couple of hours since he had last checked them. Up popped an email from Charlie:

Hi J. Just thought I'd send you a message about a possible addition to your experiment. I've discovered that a Quartz crystal has some really strange properties that are 'said' to offer many abilities to the living and beyond? Quartz has been proven with its healing properties and obviously it has very stable electrical properties. I'm thinking that if a suitable module can be constructed it might ease you into the 'other' world with grace? This would be opposed to your current method of electrocuting yourself first, to gain access.

Charlie.

Jan quickly replied, stating his interest in a safer alternative method for accessing Ivor's world. He also said that he had the funds available for Charlie to proceed - right away, with the construction of the module. Five minutes later Charlie replied:

Don't worry J, I'm already on the case, see you in the next couple of days. C.

Jan thought that with the time left before Chloe was due to be home, he would prepare dinner. *That'll please Clo,* he thought to himself.

Chloe arrived home and was delighted to see that there was a large bowl of pasta and olives waiting for her. Chloe duly filled Jan in about her training day as she tucked into her (delicious!?) pasta meal. When questioned why Jan wasn't eating as well, he replied that he had already eaten. All of a sudden, Chloe announced that she was - after all, required to stay a night in a hotel close to the training centre.

'So that would mean tomorrow night, Wednesday?'

'No. I didn't properly explain myself; it will be next Monday night. I should be back by next Tuesday evening. I'm sorry about the short notice, we didn't find out for ourselves until just before we all left-off. I'll be at work as normal tomorrow.'

It didn't take Jan very long to realise that he had a clear two-day visit to Ivor's world the following week.

The following morning. As soon as the coast was clear, Jan was back in Ivor's world.

Ivor are you there?

'Yes, I am, but please forgive me I can't remember your name.'

It's Jan. I understand Ivor, and I know that time is running out. I'm sorry that I didn't make it to see you yesterday.

'There's no such thing as a day in here Jan, and thanks for reminding me.'

Shouldn't we go to a safer place?

'Should we? I guess that you are right, Jan.'

So quickly they both headed to a Charging Chamber and Jan could once again see Ivor.

You've slightly changed again Ivor; your face is slightly different.

'Yes, I feel slightly different - certainly not like my old-self, anyway.'

You might not remember, but you said a little while ago that there might be something wrong with my blood. Well, you were right, I've had it confirmed by the doctor. He did say, however, that there was nothing to worry about.

'I guess that's okay then, just a hiccup.'

I certainly hope so! Didn't you also say that you had something to show me?

'Oh yes, it's a bit of a worrying surprise that I stumbled across. Would you like to see?'

Yeah, I think so. How long would it take to get there?

'How long have you got Jan?'

About the same as last time. Plus, a bit more.

'I don't think that will be long enough Jan.'

Well, I should have more time in a few days. Would that be, okay?

'I hope so Jan. Don't let me down, it may well be your last chance.'

No, I won't Ivor.

Jan, then left and sat for a while in the cage - tired and weak. He had only been away for a little while but felt absolutely shattered and nauseous. Finally, after a couple of hours, Jan felt able to regain his mobility again. He made his way to the house, whilst deep in thought and wishing the weekend away.

After what had seemed like a week, Monday morning had arrived - at last! It had been a difficult and long weekend for Jan and indeed for Chloe as well. They were both glad by the time Monday morning had arrived, as by now they were hardly on speaking terms with each other. Chloe left for her training early, so Jan immediately sprang into action...

Chapter Nine

Things didn't quite go as smoothly as Jan had hoped though, he spent most of Monday morning in the cage trying to contact Ivor. There was no reply, just the utter silence of the tunnel, he gave it a rest for a couple of hours, then he tried again.

Ivor, are you there?

'I'm sorry Jan, I know that you have been calling me for a long time. The thing is though, as I have already told you, I'm losing my memory very quickly now. I hardly know who I am anymore, so your calling didn't really register. I just came out of curiosity of continuously hearing your voice really. Now you are back though, some memories are glimmering back in my mind.'

I thought that might be the case. Can you still remember what you told me a few days ago about showing me something?

'Yes, I can remember that now Jan. I'm going to struggle here, but I'll try my best to explain what I would like you to know and see.'

I'm all ears Ivor - perhaps in your case though, I'm all thought.

'You see, for a while now, I've been hearing a different kind of pitch, it's getting more powerful than my usual one that I've been following for a while. It seems to resonate with me, like an angelic voice, it draws you in and makes you curious all the time to find out where it's coming from. I've been torn for a while, whether to follow it or try to stick to my own path. I'm concerned as well, that my own path will soon become too weak to follow!'

Maybe these pitches, vibrations or resonances - or whatever, only last a certain amount of time Ivor? Maybe there is a choice of destiny then, but you only get so long to choose?

'It might be the case Jan, and I did also think of this. With this in mind, I made it a priority to find the source of the sound as quickly as I could.'

Well, did you find it, and if so, what did you find Ivor?

'I will have to show you, let me take you.'

I'm ready. Let's go!

They were off again on the roller-coaster-like ride through various tunnels. Jan knew that it would take a while, so he just shut his eyes, and tried to shut his mind off from the frantic journey that they were on. *This must be similar to what astronauts have to endure, but I'm doing it in total silence. Please let it stop quickly!*

Eventually after what seemed like forever, they came to a stop. This time it was in another recharging chamber. Jan took a few seconds to recover and compose himself from what had just happened. As before, Jan could now see Ivor; however, this time Jan had to literally rub his eyes in disbelief. The sight that was before Jan's eyes was almost alien-like, even within just a few days Ivor had changed into something that was almost unrecognisable. Ivor appeared much smaller and looked quite - infantile. Nothing was obviously apparent that it was Ivor anymore. Here before Jan, was once his best friend, the grey haired, older man – albeit - once a fairly physically fit one!

'Look over there Jan.'

The tunnel entrance was fully illuminated and looked as if it was full of some kind of crystal-clear water or some other clear liquid. It exuded a rich, honey coloured glowing aura. It all seemed to defy gravity, by having a liquid surface - that was vertical?

'I don't know what the hell it is Jan, but it's so hard to not approach it and find out more? For some reason though, this is as close as we can get. The sound that I can hear though - it's like the most angelic voice I've ever heard. It's as if I'm a child again and I want my mother to pick me and for me to be in the safety of her arms again.'

Jan noticed that there were definitely more balls of light than normal around them. He also noticed that there seemed to be an invisible barrier that stopped anything getting too close to the liquid tunnel. Also, Jan realised that there was something not quite right with the tunnel, so he had to think fast to distract Ivor from obsessively trying to approach it. Quickly though, he spotted some gatekeepers in the distance, they seemed to be rapidly approaching.

Ivor, I hate to say this, but I think that we've got company!

Quickly looking in the direction of the approaching gatekeepers, Ivor took hold of Jan and led him to safety. They moved and stopped in a darker part of the tunnel, further back to an area that was more densely packed with balls of light.

Wow! there's thousands of balls of light, just hovering around. Each one, once a living physical person, who only knew the tedious monotony of going about their everyday lives.

'I don't know how much time I have left Jan? I just wanted you to know that I've enjoyed your visits, they have made it a bit more fun for me. I found it all welcome change from continuously following my path.'

Danger was getting close by now. It was like watching and waiting for a live show to start. The gatekeepers were close to the enormous gathering of balls of light. Jan could now see their features more clearly, they all looked very similar to the one that he had escaped from previously. As they continued to get closer, Jan could only now see two gatekeepers, they were very much alike: young, non-gender looking, both had long hair as well, although one had a slightly different shade of hair colour to the other one. The thing that stood out to Jan this time, was that they had no legs. In fact, Jan couldn't even define what either of them had below their waist. No matter how much he looked, he couldn't make out any shape or form. In the end he put the failure down to himself still having physical eyes?

The two gatekeepers seemed to hang around for what seemed hours. Jan looked down at his watch, he thought to himself: *I can see the time, but I haven't got a clue what day it is?* At the same time Ivor eased himself and Jan further back from the gatekeepers, who were turning their attention to the liquid tunnel as they approached it. Suddenly Jan felt a cold presence close to his ear. A voice whispered in Jan's ear:

'GOING SOMEWHERE?'

Almost immediately, Jan was hurtling through the tunnels again, at a faster, more hectic rate. They stopped in another chamber; this wasn't good though as yet more gatekeepers were already there. One of them was 'really' close and immediately reached out to touch Jan - who could start to feel the pain of ultra-coldness as the gatekeeper's hand drew closer to him. Instantly, Jan and Ivor were on their way again. They stopped in another chamber, this time there was nothing! Only deep, deep coldness, or - that's what it felt like to Jan anyway!

'We can't stay here for long Jan!'

I'm in agreement Ivor, this place feels like it's sucking all the energy out of me with this painful, numb coldness!

'It's the same for me Jan, we need to get out of here - fast! I'll have to take us back to the first chamber, hopefully the gatekeepers have gone.'

Ivor grabbed hold of Jan - again. Nothing happened though - this time. The oppressive coldness had drawn a lot of energy from Ivor, rendering him incapable of taking them both into a high-speed getaway.

'It's no good Jan, we'll have to try and make it over to a tunnel, then we might be able to get on our way.'

It was as if Ivor was in 'limp' mode; the pace was painfully slow. Luckily, the nearest tunnel wasn't too much further. Upon arriving and looking into the tunnel, Jan looked around and noticed an immediate problem - fast approaching!

It's a bloody gatekeeper Ivor, and he's moving pretty quickly - this way!

They managed to enter the tunnel though, before the gatekeeper got too close. They were on their way again, however, not at the usual rapid pace, but enough to keep ahead of the pursuing gatekeeper.

'I'm taking us back to the first chamber Jan.'

What the hell for Ivor?

'It's the only way that I can think of to get a quick feed of energy.'

It took a while but eventually they arrived back at the first tunnel. The atmosphere had now changed, the angelic hum was now quite loud - but it was very warm and had an audible tube smoothness to it. The gatekeepers were still there and presided over the entrance to the liquid tunnel, which was now displaying a bubble-like quality to the liquid. As they drew even closer, they could see that the gatekeepers were guiding balls of light into the tunnel, many at a time.

What is going on - what are they doing Ivor? Is this some kind of processing chamber?

It was too late! as Jan turned to Ivor, he just caught the last part of Ivor's manifestation into a ball of light. Ivor's ball of light then seemed to automatically move into line with the other balls of light moving towards the liquid tunnel. Unfortunately, and unknowingly for Jan, Ivor had fallen under the spell of the tunnel and he had tricked Jan to go back - this was unavoidable for Ivor! He had to now face his 'ultimate' destiny.

Jan was now trapped and stuck to the spot without Ivor. Luckily for him though he still had the panic button! He pressed it. Everything went immediately black!

Several days later, he came around on the floor of the cage. His first thoughts were of wanting to 'really' die. He was in pain, muscles spasmed, he was throwing up, his mouth was full of ulcers and his skin was cracking and bleeding. He managed to find a drink of water from an old plastic bottle sitting on his desk, also - somehow, he managed to stand up, he started to make his way back to the house. Once inside he dragged himself into the kitchen. There on the worktop stood up a note - Jan didn't really need to open it up to read what it said as he was almost certain of its handwritten content:

Like the addiction of a drug user, you're hooked to that machine. You have let me down and I'm fearing where it is all heading for us? I'm staying at Ellen's for now. DO NOT attempt to contact me, until YOU have cleaned yourself up!

Jan threw the note back onto the worktop, that's when he noticed a cardboard box, also on the worktop. It was addressed to himself. Unpacking the contents - it then clicked, it was the Quartz module together with a note from Charlie. He gave it a brief inspection whilst chuckling to himself at the same time and thinking to himself: *I wonder? Will this do anything? Will it do what I think it might do?* He couldn't really give it anymore thought in the state that he was in, so he pushed the module and the note to one side and headed upstairs.

With only some water at his bedside Jan slept for - what seemed like days. Every time he awoke, he still didn't feel as if he had the strength to arise from his bed though. However, after a few more days he started to feel a bit more like his old-self and felt like he might have enough energy to attempt a descent on the stairs. Amazingly, once he made it to the kitchen, he did make himself a cup of tea and a couple of slices of toast, unfortunately though, these were forgotten about once he started to inspect his new gadget.

As the day moved on, Jan sat down and thought about his situation. He felt pretty bad about letting Chloe down, but he assumed that after a few more days she would have calmed down a bit. With this, he shuffled that problem to the 'sorted' part of his mind. He was very confused about Ivor though. Did Ivor die again - twice? Should he mourn for Ivor again? The fact was that he was too far-gone to really care. He wanted to be back in 'that world' again, free from all physical restrictions and responsibilities. Only the strength of love for his wife would make him stay, however, she wasn't around, and the urge to fit the Quartz module was - at this minute, the strongest urge inside him. He then remembered that he had not yet read Charlie's note. He picked up the note that was in with the module, it read:

Hi Jan. I hope that you are well. Please, be aware that the Quartz module is very, very fragile and will probably need some kind of damping with foam or such-like, to keep it as stable as possible. I have no idea what you can expect from this module – maybe, nothing at all?

Take care, hope to see you soon. C.

Jan laid the note down, gathered up the module and headed down to the lab. Once in the lab he set about installing the module into a port slot on the test rig. However, unlike before when he was setting up the rig and cage, he now was not-so focused, or hardly up to the delicate task at hand. Having accessed the port slots on the rig, he fumbled with the module, eventually finding any old slot in which to insert it. Pushing it home, the need to secure it didn't even come across his mind - let alone fitting some sort of damping material. *There, all done. Now to fire it all up and see what she can do now?*

Chapter Ten

'Do you think that I should give Jan a call, or go and see if he's alright Ellen?'

'It's only been a few day's Clo, if you make contact with him now, it'll just end up in a shouting match. Make him sweat and fend for himself for a bit longer, so that he can fully appreciate what you mean to him and what he has to lose if you were to properly leave.'

'I'm quite worried about him as it wasn't that long ago that I had to get our neighbour to pick Jan off from the floor of that cage.'

'I should think that he is fine Clo, the bedroom light was on as well as other house lights when we rode past last night. He's probably lying-in bed right now, feeling sorry for himself and gathering up the courage to give you a call. Why don't you give him a little longer to gather his thoughts - maybe for a few more days? Then if he hasn't called you, take him by surprise by paying a visit?'

'Yeah, I think you're right Elle.'

Back in the lab, Jan was in the cage and sitting ready, and waiting to go back to Ivor's world. He flicked the switch - it went dark for a split second then all of a sudden, he found himself back in a tunnel. He couldn't believe his eyes! Gone was the dark tunnel interior, it was still dark but it glowed all over in the darkest deep tones of colour that he had ever seen. The colours were even-in-brightness, and had a wonderful three-dimensional depth to them. Suddenly, a golden light flashed past Jan, he stepped back. *Hang on,* he thought to himself. *What? I can move around and walk all by myself! This is bizarre!* Another light flashed by, this time he could make out more of the features. The features of these lights looked very similar to how Ivor had appeared to Jan. *This is surreal, I could only see them as balls of light before - but now, I can see them in their full spirit form. I'm guessing that Charlie was right about the Quartz!*

Jan stood around for a little while just taking it all in. Several more spirits went by, none of them seemed to notice Jan though, so he decided to try something. After a short while of waiting to try it out, he saw another spirit approaching. He then stepped into the direct path of the oncoming spirit, he shut his eyes, then - nothing. It passed straight through him. *I guess that means I'm still alive then.* He walked tentatively on, burdened, but kind of pleased with himself that he was 'probably' the only physical person to have visited, and to have walked in the spirit world - all by himself.

As he moved on, he thought that it would only be right, and to honour Ivor, if he tried to find the processing chamber - maybe he could find out what 'did' happen to Ivor? As he moved slowly on his way, he kept on shouting Ivor's name inside his head. He knew though, that there was no real chance of receiving a reply. Maybe the reason for his calling was to dampen his slight nervousness at being able to search this world at will - like someone who has just passed their driving test and is venturing out on their own for the first time.

Progress was slow for Jan, it was sort of like - walking along a main road - in the middle, although in some ways, much safer.

At last, he came upon a chamber, so he entered. It was bright and clear, just like he had always seen it, only this time, the tunnel entrances were all lit - just like the tunnel that he had walked along. The other tunnels weren't the same colour though, some were blues and reds, some though, had a multi-coloured fuzzy snow appearance. Jan couldn't look at these ones for very long though, as the intensity of the light made his eyes ache after a bit, so he decided to make his way to the centre of the chamber. Something didn't seem quite right though, as he drew closer to the centre, some gatekeepers started to appear - what seemed to be on a mini horizon. It was as if he was walking over the brow of a hill and was starting to see what was on the other side, but the floor seemed to be flat and level? This utterly panicked Jan, he frantically looked around for somewhere to hide, it was too late though, the gatekeepers were too close for him to remain unseen. Jan froze with fear, the gatekeepers quickly looked Jan's way, but strangely they appeared to look straight through him. He just stood there waiting for them to approach, then, three of them started to head Jan's way. He thought to himself: *This is it!* He shut his eyes and knelt down, a few seconds later he opened his eyes again and looked forward - then back. Astonishingly, the gatekeepers had gone straight past Jan. *I can't believe it,* he thought to himself.

He decided to shout it out:

'I CAN'T BELIEVE IT!'

'I CAN'T BELIEVE IT!'

'I CAN'T BELIEVE IT!'

Cowering down, he waited for the repercussion of his outburst, would the gatekeepers return instantly and take him away? No, there was nothing. *Can I be led to think that I have the freedom of this place, to come and go as I please with the freedom of a ghost or spirit - within this spirit world? That's impossible - surely!*

With renewed vigour Jan walked on to the outer edge of the chamber, it took a while but eventually he reached the collection of tunnel entrances. *This is great! Which one shall I choose?* He almost couldn't stop himself from chuckling. *I know, I'll try the red tunnel.*

It's amazing how quickly someone's confidence can receive a boost once they are in possession of the knowledge - that they probably won't get caught.

This tunnel was different - in the fact that there were much fewer spirits following their destiny paths, it had a different feeling as well. Jan thought that it was a bit colder and slightly more oppressive than the first one. He put that down to the audible pitch and the kind of spirit that was destined to pass through. A while later he recognised the brightness illuminating from the end of the tunnel. *Ah, another chamber if I'm not mistaken,* he thought to himself. This chamber was pretty much the same as the last, although Jan did spot a far-off tunnel entrance that was dark. Jan being Jan though, and together with his renewed confidence, he headed straight for the dark tunnel. The entrance seemed a bit larger than normal and on further inspection Jan could hear a faint sound coming from deep within the tunnel.

He stood for quite a while just carefully listening. This wasn't, and also at the same time - was, a hard task in this - the quietest place that he had ever been to. However, he couldn't quickly make his mind up, whether to venture inside - or not? In the end he couldn't resist as curiosity got the better of him.

If anyone of us 'normal' folk were to be asked the question: "If you could visit the afterlife, would you expect anything that you see to be solid to the touch?" Most - at a guess, would say no - one would expect? That is what surprised Jan, because on his previous visits with Ivor he couldn't even remember feeling anything that had any solidity. Ever since the start of his solo journey, though, everything that he had felt, either whilst walking or touching had a flexible, but a degree of solidity to it. Every surface that he touched or walked on was solid, but - with a bit of give. Jan inched into the tunnel entrance, it was still dark, but there was a faint glow at a distance, this becoming more visible as he moved slowly along inside the tunnel. This tunnel to him, out of all of them, seemed to lack any kind of feeling or impression on his senses. The other noticeable thing apparent, once he started to move along it, was that this tunnel was quite bendy in comparison with all the others.

All of a sudden and without no time to take action, two lights flew past him at high speed. Jan ducked down - much too late though, as they already passed over him! He carried on, moving slowly. A little further on in the tunnel, the same thing happened again, as before, they flew straight over the top of him, four lights this time! Jan picked up his pace as much as he could. The light source got a bit brighter and within a little while he could see that it was another tunnel entrance. Now he felt quite confident that he was safe - he stood in front of the entrance.

Inside, there was another room, and all around were gatekeepers - maybe twenty or more, all motionless, as if they were sleeping or meditating. In the middle of the room, he saw what he could only describe as a puddle of liquid. It didn't look like water - more like molten metal or mercury, but a much more reflective surface, like a liquid mirror perhaps? Jan stood and watched for some time, there was absolutely no movement at all, until two of the gatekeepers suddenly became alert and moved towards the puddle. They both bent down and touched the liquid, they then moved towards the tunnel entrance. Having exited the room, they instantly took off in flight down the tunnel. Jan stopped for a bit to have a think about what he had just seen: *Knowing that the gatekeepers have total control here, I'm guessing that room is some kind of recharging area, and touching the liquid gave them their orders - maybe?*

Knowing that he would never probably know the answer, he moved on further down the tunnel. It still induced the same feelings into Jan, however, there was no gatekeeper traffic.

Quite a while later, still in the same tunnel, Jan was more or less trudging along. It was pitch black - he had to stop. He gave a thought to himself: *There could be a very good reason behind the lack of gatekeepers in this part of the tunnel. There probably isn't an exit?* Without further hesitation he turned around and started to move back along the way he came.

After what seemed like an age, he finally jumped - well stumbled, back into the chamber which he was previously in. Hardly having any energy left to sit up from his stumble, he decided to rest a bit. He shut his eyes and a complex thought approached him: *Is it possible to sleep in the spirit world?* Well, after trying very hard - he didn't! He just relaxed until he felt that he could move on again.

Getting up and unsure what to do next, he noticed one of the eye-aching fuzzy light tunnels. He was cautious about staring at it for any length of time, as he remembered the last time, he saw one of them it started to induce a headache. However, this time he realised that he could now look at it just the same way as he could at all the other tunnel entrances. Curiosity drew him towards it. He reached out his hand to place it inside the tunnel entrance, instantly, his hand felt as if every relaxation method known was being applied to it. He had never felt anything like this before, the entrance had also now changed its luminance. Where once before it had resembled a rave light show, it was now emitting a weird soft white ring of light. This ring of light was continuous along the tunnel as far as he could see - like a tunnel within a tunnel. Jan didn't hesitate to enter. The feeling once he stepped in - felt life changing! He couldn't even compute it in his mind. Imagine having a glass of good wine whilst getting in a lovely deep warm bath after having the best massage ever - well forget that! This was one thousand levels - at least, above.

He carried on moving through the tunnel, grinning and feeling so full of energy and fitness, together with an overwhelming feeling of youth - with the pace to match. *Am I drunk, or am I dreaming? Perhaps I'm both,* he couldn't stop saying to himself.

He came to the end of the tunnel and felt as if he had almost skipped out into the chamber. Standing in the chamber, he felt very happy and quite at peace with everything. He then realised that this chamber was where he had wanted to be anyway: the 'liquid tunnel' chamber. Unfortunately, the sight of a gatekeeper also standing close to the liquid tunnel entrance unsettled Jan a bit. He was still quite confident though, so he made his way towards the tunnel. There was no avoiding the gatekeeper on the way though, Jan thought to himself: *Not a problem! They aren't going to have any idea that I'm even nearby.* Slowly he walked past the gatekeeper, who didn't flinch or say a word.

'That's where you are wrong Jan.'

Jan stopped without saying anything.

'Going somewhere?'

Jan looked down for the panic button. It was gone!

Eh, uh, I was going to look at that strange watery tunnel thing there.

'Be my guest,' said the gatekeeper looking away, with what seemed a slight smirk. The gatekeeper then looked back at Jan, and softly spoke:

'Welcome to - Hell.'

Jan looked at the entrance to the liquid tunnel, which had now quickly changed to a more orangery tone. Jan looked back at the gatekeeper, then he looked forward again. He then made his way to 'His' destiny…

***

It was breakfast time back at Ellen's together with her new short-term tenant - Chloe.

'I think that it's time I checked up on Jan, what do you think Ellen?'

'Yes, I agree. I thought he might have attempted to make some kind of contact with you by now. He must be starving? Tell you what, I know that it's only a few doors away, but we'll take the car in case anything gets out of hand.'

'It'll save my embarrassment from the neighbours as well. We'll go after we've finished breakfast - yeah?' They finished up, washed up, and they both hopped into the car.

'You okay Clo?'

'Yes, I'm fine Elle - why has everything got a strange look, and why do I feel different?'

Ten seconds later, they arrived outside Chloe's house.

'Do you want me to wait here Clo?'

'Please, if you would, then it will look like we are on our way out somewhere after I've seen Jan.'

Chloe turned the key in the front door and opened it. She entered inside and slowly walked around downstairs. Nothing had changed much since she was last there. *He's either not here or he's become very tidy all of a sudden.* She then walked upstairs, the bed was unmade, everything else looked all in order. *He's not even here, where the hell has he gone?*

Chloe made her way back to the car.

'That was quick Clo, how did you get on - did you see him?'

'No, I didn't, that's the strange thing Elle.'

'What about his lab thingy, did you check in there?' Chloe shut the car door and made her way to the lab. As she got close to the lab, she could hear the industrial sound of the coils chuffing away. *This is unbelievable,* she thought. *Has he really not got any idea!*

Walking through the door, she instantly set eyes upon him … his lifeless body was laid out on the floor of the cage.

THE END